THE ECO-KIDS

THE CLEAN-UP CREW

KATHRYN MAKRIS is the author of seventeen Young Adult and middle grades novels, including the AL-MOST SISTERS series and CROSSTOWN from Avon Books.

As a reporter, Kathryn has covered hurricanes, capital murder trials, and Lego contests. She has hosted a radio talk show and has interviewed national personalities including the Rev. Jesse Jackson, Sissy Spacek, the real "Colonel" Sanders, and Benji the dog.

Raised in Texas in a family that spoke Greek and Spanish along with English, Kathryn now thrives on California's mix of cultures. She also enjoys flamenco dance, dogs, and almost anything outdoors.

This book is dedicated to ''eco-kids'' everywhere

Thanks to the Peninsula Conservation Center in Palo Alto, California, and the Santa Clara County Manufacturing Group in Santa Clara, California, publishers of *The Recycling Partnership for Schools & Businesses,* a treasure of information.

1

At just three minutes before 8 A.M., Jess McCabe slid into a seat in the second row from the front of the classroom. The first row was already taken. She had never been so late to school in her life, a fact she pointed out to her friend Sienna Sabo. It was all her fault.

Sienna rolled her eyes. "We're not late, for heaven's sake. We're early. Class starts at eight."

"To me, this is late." Jess pulled her binder out of her tote bag and opened it to the section for English class. It was neatly marked in capital letters on a yellow tab, the color Jess always used for English. There were only a few pages of work in the binder, it being only the third day of seventh grade. From the pen and pencil compartment of her bag Jess chose a blue medium ballpoint, clicked it open, and sat ready for class to begin.

"Late is *after* eight o'clock," said Sienna from the desk behind her.

Jess turned around. "Late is when you have to run to get here. Late is when you come through the door huffing and puffing and don't get the seat you want. We were late."

Sienna rolled her eyes again and pushed back her

long reddish curls. That hair was one of the reasons why Sienna had kept Jess and their friend Cary Chen waiting for ten minutes that morning. Sienna had tried on four different headbands. Other reasons included Sienna's red Western boots, which she had changed out of and back into twice, and Sienna's Western-style outfit, including fringed suede jacket, white skirt, and red tights. It had started out as a peasant look then mutated before Jess's and Cary's eyes into something from Sienna's idea of a ranch.

By the time they finally got Sienna out her front door it was 7:46. Thank goodness Jewel Beach Junior High was only a few blocks down Opal Street.

"If I went preppie every day like you do, it wouldn't take me very long to get ready, either," Sienna proclaimed, giving Jess's pink button-down shirt and khaki pants a sideways glance. "Doesn't take much imagination."

"There is nothing wrong with wearing sensible clothes," countered Jess, "or with not being a fashion hound like you."

Sienna put a hand on her hip. "I am not a fashion hound. I just like to express myself through what I wear."

Jess rolled her eyes. Sienna saw getting dressed as an art project. Jess, on the other hand, felt that the less time wasted on it, the better. In fact, she had arranged her own clothes into sets so that it took approximately one and one-half minutes to dress in the morning. From the second her alarm went off at 6:45 on school days, to the second she walked out the door to meet Cary on the sidewalk, it took no more than fifty minutes.

That morning, for example, she had rolled out of bed,

2

dressed, washed her face, and checked her dark brown skin for the zits she knew would eventually come, now that she was twelve. Zero so far. By then it was 6:58. Then she worked her long black hair into two braids, crisscrossed them over the top of her head, pinned them, and slipped on her glasses. Five after seven, right on schedule. Twenty-five minutes for breakfast, five minutes brushing her teeth and pulling on her shoes, then out the door right on time at 7:35.

Sienna's mind-set, to say the least, was different. As usual, their conversation about clothing had gotten them nowhere. Jess sighed and gave up. She glanced toward the next row at Cary, whose shiny black cap of hair bounced as she talked with the girl in front of her. Cary hadn't put a word in during Jess's argument with Sienna. It seemed she never got involved in their disagreements anymore. In the past, she had always said something soothing or changed the subject for them.

The bell rang. Mr. Gormley, the school principal, made a few uninteresting announcements on the loudspeaker. After calling the roll, Ms. Toshimi told the class, ''Today we'll perform one of American education's classic exercises. We are going to talk about our summer vacations. The idea for this exercise is to help develop our public speaking skills. It will also help us get to know one another a little, won't it?''

To set an example, Ms. Toshimi went first, describing her two-week trip to Lake Havasu for house-boating and waterskiing. Then she talked about a poetry course she'd taken at the local college, pointing out that teachers had to learn just as students did.

Jess chewed on her pen cap. Public speaking gave her the willies.

"Now, in case anyone noticed," Ms. Toshimi said, "my talk ran just under two minutes. That's how much time you'll each get, too. The idea is to stay relaxed and natural. Just chat with us and hold our interest, as if you're talking with a friend. All right? Let's start over here on this side." She pointed to the other side of the room.

Four rows away, Jess breathed a sigh of relief. At least she'd have some time to prepare. It seemed like no time at all, though, before Sienna's turn came up. Jess's would be next. And by that time, Sienna would probably have told the whole story of the very unusual summer that she, Jess and Cary had spent together.

"Hi! I'm Sienna Sabo!" Flashing her pretty smile, Sienna took immediate command of the class's attention. Her bright, cheery voice filled the room.

There was Sienna for you, thought Jess. Loved the spotlight. Jess looked at her watch. Ms. Toshimi would have a hard time holding her to two minutes.

"I had a great summer vacation," Sienna bubbled. As she talked she made sweeping gestures through the air with her long, graceful arms. "My friends and I started a club to help animals. We're called the Five Cat Club, because we started by taking care of five abandoned kittens. But the greatest thing we did was—" She paused and took a breath, having the effect of a drum roll. "We were on TV!"

"Wait a minute," the teacher interrupted. "You weren't the ones who—?"

"Freed the Aquarius dolphins!" Sienna nodded. "That's us."

Ms. Toshimi grinned. "Of course! I remember the news stories."

4

A boy in the back of the class piped up with, "I saw you on the news."

Sienna smiled wide. "Channel Six."

"Cary and Jess? You were involved, too, weren't you?" asked Ms. Toshimi.

The girls nodded.

Ms. Toshimi grinned again. "Well, for Pete's sake. How exciting. I hadn't made the connection with your names."

Sienna added, "Later, two more people joined. Two boys."

"Your *boyfriends?*" Derek Han grinned.

"No!" Sienna shrieked. "No way! Just Ramon Sanchez and Webb Marsh from our old school. We each kept one kitten."

"Are you trying to say you run an animal rights group?" asked a boy with the uncommon name of Freedom Sutter.

Sienna shrugged. "I don't know. I guess so. I mean, we saved the kittens and the dolphins. And three puppies that somebody abandoned on Cary's doorstep. She kept one of them and his name is Bal, and Ramon got one and we found a good home for the other, so—"

"Hmph." Freedom scowled. "Takes a lot more than that if you really care about animals."

Jess swallowed. Great, just great—a heckler. As if having to get up and talk weren't bad enough! And what on earth did Freedom mean by that remark?

"Now, now," said Ms. Toshimi. "Let's not harass the speakers. Keep your questions courteous. Please continue, Sienna."

"Well, the way we did it," Sienna plunged on, "is we went to Aquarius Marine Park, where they were

5

keeping these two dolphins. It's the kind of place where they have exhibits of all kinds of fish and sea lions and dolphins, and a water-ski show and stuff. It's kind of half zoo, half circus. Fun to go to, in a way. But we found out that two of the dolphins, Leon and Tamara, had been captured in the wild. I mean, like, kidnapped from the ocean. We didn't think it was right to keep wild dolphins locked up in small pools and make them do tricks and stuff, so we tried to talk to the Aquarius company about it on the phone and in a letter. But they wouldn't pay any attention to us.''

Sienna's hazel eyes narrowed to slits. She crossed her arms and tapped a foot, the picture of anger and impatience, exactly the emotions that members of the Five Cat Club had experienced toward the Aquarius Marine Park that summer.

Ms. Toshimi and the class chuckled at Sienna's dramatics.

''So''—Sienna broke into a sly grin—''we made it so they *had* to pay attention.''

''I saw you in the newspaper. You held a protest, right?'' asked the blond girl in front of Cary.

Sienna clasped her hands together to pantomime holding up a protest sign. She marched back and forth in front of the class. ''We made signs asking Aquarius to please talk with us, and we carried them on the sidewalk in front of the Aquarius gates. We were very peaceful and quiet. But that didn't stop Aquarius from sending the cops out to bust us.''

''Cool!'' remarked Derek. A moment before he had been doodling in his notebook. Now he was all ears.

''We should say 'police officers' rather than 'cops,' '' interjected Ms. Toshimi.

6

"These weren't really cop—I mean police officers," Sienna explained. "They were security guards, and they tried to chase us away. But Cary's big brother defended us." Sienna's voice went dreamy, as it always did when the subject was Buck. "He is so wonderful. He told them we had every right to be there and they couldn't stop us. To prove his point we all sat down and held a sit-in."

"Excuse me, Sienna," Ms. Toshimi cut in. "I'm sorry to report that your two minutes are up. You've given us a thoroughly entertaining look at your lively summer. Maybe Jess will want to continue the story."

After Sienna nodded and sat down, Jess stood up. She cleared her throat. "Yes, I do. But—" Nervously, she cleared her throat again. Public speaking was definitely Sienna's strong point, not hers. "Well, I disagree with Sienna on at least one issue. Which is, well, I don't think appearing on TV was the best thing we accomplished, though it probably was what got the most attention." She took a breath and tried to organize her thoughts.

"What happened after the sit-in?" Freedom asked. "What did the security guards do?"

"Oh." Jess nodded. At least he was being polite now. "Well, right after we sat down a TV news crew showed up. You know Freddy Fredemeyer on Channel Six? It's kind of a long story, but we had met him during our visit to Aquarius a week or two earlier, and later we had called to let him know we were going to hold the protest. As soon as the security guards spotted his camera they took off. They don't care for bad publicity. Our protest was shown on TV, and pretty soon after that

Aquarius asked a wildlife group to help them rehabilitate the dolphins.''

"Re-what?" asked Derek.

"Rehabilitation. It means helping them learn to be wild again. Leon and Tamara are in a special habitat in Florida now, learning all over again how to hunt fish and interact with other wild dolphins and avoid predators, so that maybe they can be returned to the open ocean someday.''

The blond girl in front of Cary raised her hand. "What are dolphins' predators?"

"Sharks. And orcas, also called killer whales. And, of course, humans." Jess adjusted her glasses, getting more and more excited. "To me the most important aspect of our summer was not so much what we did as what we learned." Her head tilted sideways. She felt a brightness inside and was no longer the least bit nervous. "There's so much I didn't know before all this happened. We learned about a wildlife group, the Southern California Marine Mammal Association, that helps rescue dolphins. They're the ones who took Leon and Tamara to the safety area in Florida. Oh, and here's a puzzle for you. How many adult cats does it take to produce eighty million kittens?"

"Eighty million kittens?" Ms. Toshimi repeated.

Jess nodded.

"Hmm," said Hallie Greer. "Let's see. If there are about five kittens in a litter, and two parents to every litter, divide five into eighty million, multiply that by two . . ." She did some quick arithmetic on her notepad. "Thirty-two million?"

Jess shook her head. "Guess again. The answer is . . . two.''

"Two million?" asked Ms. Toshimi.

"No. Not two million. Just two. Two cats." Jess smiled. "In just ten years, two cats and their offspring and the offspring of their offspring can add up to the millions."

"Wow. You mean my kitty, Ringer, can have that many great-great-great grandkittens that fast?" asked Malcolm Palmer, another student from their school last year.

"If you let her," Jess warned, "yes, very easily."

With that, Jess's time was up. But Ms. Toshimi let Cary go next so that she could fill in the rest of the girls' summer story.

Jess sat back in her chair and tried to settle down. She felt flushed and excited and would have loved to talk about scientific things all day. Maybe that's what it would be like to be a biologist or an animal behaviorist, getting together with other scientists to discuss important ideas and findings.

Cary talked about what would happen to Ringer's kittens and grandkittens and great grandkittens—how very few of them would find homes, how seventeen million dogs and cats were put to sleep every year because there were just too many of them.

"The only way to stop this," Cary went on, "is by spaying and neutering your pets. Those are easy operations that make it so they can't have kittens or puppies. And one of the things our club did over the summer was try to spread the word about that. We started a pet care hot line at my house, where we answer questions on the phone. We tell people about spaying and neutering and other things, too. This one guy wanted to

9

know how to tell a male from a female goldfish, and a woman asked me how to brush a goat.''

Everybody laughed.

''But the important thing we try to get across is that animals have the right to good lives. They can feel love and hurt just like people. And, well . . .'' Cary's dark eyes got misty. She pushed her hair behind her ears. ''See, the way our club got its name is that each of our five members kept one kitten from that litter we found abandoned in the vacant lot in our neighborhood. The kittens were only a few days old. They couldn't even see or crawl yet. They had been stuffed into a paper sack and tossed into a trash pile. Somebody had just thrown them away.'' Cary bit her lip. ''When I think about what would have happened to my kitten, Tolkien, if we hadn't found him and his brothers and sisters, I feel really sad and scared. Kittens and puppies and other animals really need our help. That was the most important thing I learned this summer.''

Jess thought she heard Ms. Toshimi sniffle a little. In fact, she had to sniff back a tear herself, thinking about what might have happened to her own kitten, Tolkien's sister Curie, if she hadn't been rescued from that trash heap.

''Well, you girls had quite an interesting summer,'' said Ms. Toshimi, ''and it made for three excellent presentations. We'll look forward to hearing more about your club in the future.''

''Oh, you will!'' Sienna nodded. ''We've got lots going on!''

· Jess smiled. It was a good bet they'd hear from Sienna whether they wanted to or not.

After English, Jess had two other classes before noon.

10

So far she loved junior high. Switching from room to room for each class, getting to know different teachers . . . Plus, she had made it into the gifted program's math and science classes, which were much more interesting than her classes in elementary school. By lunchtime her stomach was grumbling. Entering the cafeteria, her ears started ringing, too. The Jewel Beach Junior High cafeteria was much noisier than the one at Jewel Beach Elementary had been. Jess glanced up at the ceiling to see what might be different about the two rooms. This ceiling did seem a little lower. And the floor was ceramic tile instead of linoleum. Maybe that made a difference. Probably what made the biggest difference, though, was the fact that the junior high had a few hundred more students than the elementary school, Jess realized. More kids meant more noise.

"What are you frowning about?" someone asked, poking her in the ribs.

Jess turned to find Ramon Sanchez next to her. "I wasn't frowning. I was thinking."

"You're always thinking, McCabe," he said, following her to the table that she and her friends had claimed as their own. No one else was there yet. "What an amazing brain you are." He made a cross-eyed face.

"Thank you," Jess answered calmly. Being calm around Ramon was not always easy, but getting to know him over the summer had helped. He and Webb Marsh, who now attended another school, were the two male members of the Five Cat Club.

"So when's the next Five Cat meeting going to be?" Ramon asked, dragging a comb through his curly black hair.

11

"We discussed that at the last meeting. You were there," Jess told him.

Ramon shrugged. "I forgot."

Jess pulled her pocket datebook out of her tote bag. "You should write it down next time. Like this." She showed him the entry for Saturday, September 11. *Five Cat Club 2 P.M. Cary Chen's house.*

"Hi, folks!" Cary greeted them as she walked up. "How'd you do on the California history quiz, Ramon?" She sat down next to Jess.

"Massacre," he answered.

"It got you, huh?" asked Jess.

"Nope," Cary answered for him. "Ramon's great at history."

"I aced it. Yours isn't the only brain in the world, you know, McCabe." Ramon bared his teeth at her.

Jess nodded and smiled. "Just the best. Why don't you stop standing there and sit down already, Ramon? Stop hovering."

Ramon backed up half a step. "Nah. I'm, uh, sitting somewhere else."

Cary rolled her eyes. "Aw, just sit down, Ramon. It's not going to kill you. You hung out with us all summer, for heaven's sake."

He backed up another step, waving good-bye.

Jess shook her head. "Sitting with girls at lunch isn't socially acceptable, I suppose."

Just as he turned to go, Sienna strolled up and set her things on the table. "Phew! I thought P.E. would never end. Fifteen push-ups! Hi, everybody!"

"Ramon refuses to sit with us," Cary reported, pointing at the frozen-looking boy behind her.

12

"Be cool, Ramon," Sienna counseled. "Come on. This is junior high, not Jewel Beach Elementary."

To Jess's astonishment, Ramon called back, "Thanks, anyway," in a polite tone. He shuffled off and found a spot at a table full of boys.

"Well, I guess that's a safe enough distance from us." Sienna shrugged.

Jess and Cary joined her in a giggle. Boys could be so weird.

After lunch boys began to seem even weirder, because as Jess and the others threw their paper sacks into the trash bin at the back of the cafeteria, one boy suddenly yelled out, "Hey!" and caught Sienna's sack in midair. He opened it, peered inside, then emptied its entire contents on a nearby table.

"What are you doing?" Jess demanded. She realized the boy was Freedom Sutter, their classmate from English.

"If you wanted my leftovers, all you had to do was ask," Sienna told him.

Freedom was still poking through her trash. "*Hmm.*"

"*Hmm* what?" asked Cary.

Freedom shook his head, a long blond mop. "One empty plastic pudding cup. Half a sandwich. Tuna."

"Chicken salad," Sienna corrected.

"One banana peel, one candy wrapper . . ." he continued.

"Is this some kind of joke?" Sienna asked.

Freedom pushed the hair away from his eyes. "Well, you claim you love animals."

"What does that have to do with Sienna's trash?" Cary wanted to know.

Ramon strolled up. "Lose a contact, Sutter?"

13

"Let's look at yours." Freedom grabbed Ramon's sack out of his hands.

"Hey, what're you doing?" Ramon tried to snatch it back.

By then Freedom had already emptied it out next to Sienna's. "Why did you pack this orange if you weren't going to eat it?"

"My mother packed it," Ramon said.

"Do you need all this plastic wrap on your sandwich? You could have used a reusable container. Or aluminum foil and reused it, then recycled it."

"What is this—an ecology lesson?" Ramon growled. "Who made you the trash police?"

Freedom shrugged. "In English class *they*"—he pointed a finger at Jess, Sienna, and Cary—"talked about your club and how you want to help animals. Well, I'm here to tell you something. Trash dumps do *not* help animals."

2

For a few seconds, while Freedom's words sank in, no one said anything.

Then Jess repeated, "Trash dumps?"

Freedom nodded. "Public dumps are getting full, and cities have to take over land for new ones. If animals are living there they end up homeless. Deer, raccoons, birds, whatever. And dumps sometimes cause pollution, too. That's not any better for wildlife than it is for humans."

"Well, what are we supposed to do with our garbage?" Sienna frowned. "Not throw it away? Take it home? Then what?"

"What you can do," Freedom answered, "is make less of it. Recycle more, use less wrapping. . . ."

"We recycle our soft drink cans at home," Cary offered. "My little brother takes them to his scout troop's recycling program every week. But there's no place to recycle here at school."

"You could carry your cans home from lunch, couldn't you?" Freedom challenged her. "I do."

"Well, aren't you just so special." Ramon wagged his head back and forth.

Jess tapped a finger on her chin. "You believe there's

a connection between our creating trash and the problems of animals.''

"Everything is connected," replied Freedom.

Wearing a SAVE THE REDWOODS T-shirt and patched blue jeans, he looked like some environmentalists Jess had seen on TV recently. Her father had laughed and called them ''tree huggers'' because they chained themselves to centuries-old redwoods to keep loggers from cutting them down.

"You're hypocritical," Freedom went on, "if you say you want to help animals, but you don't care about poisoning their planet."

"Hey, it's my planet, too," Ramon objected.

"Right," agreed Freedom, "so why do you want to ruin it?''

Sienna shook her head at him. "Nobody said we did.''

"I'm very interested in helping the environment," added Cary.

Freedom shrugged. "Then get smart." He picked her empty drink can out of the trash and tossed it to her. "Think about it.''

Cary barely caught the can, dotted with potato chips and sandwich remains. "Yuck.''

"Hmph!" Sienna snorted. "Of all the nerve!''

"What a know-it-all," echoed Ramon.

Jess gazed at Cary's slimy soda can, still thinking about Freedom's challenge. It seemed to her that the Five Cat Club would have something new to discuss at their next meeting.

On Saturday the five members of the club sat around Cary's kitchen table. Sunshine streamed in through the

16

window over the sink, and the open door to the backyard let in a light breeze.

The door also let in a variety of noises: the shrieking of Cary's little brother, Luke, and his small army of friends; the barking of the Chen family dogs, Lucille and Bal, playing with Ramon's dog Lefty, who he had brought over to visit his doggy brother. Then there was the noise from Cary's older brother and his friends *inside* the house. Buck's stereo was located all the way upstairs, but in the kitchen Jess could hear the pounding rock music beat loud and clear.

"Everything is connected," she was trying to say over the noise. "Remember when Freedom said that? Well, that's actually a basic principle of ecology. I read about it in one of the pamphlets from the Southern California Marine Mammal Association."

"What does it mean?" asked Webb Marsh in his quiet voice. Even when there wasn't much background noise, Jess sometimes had to strain to hear Webb. In spite of his tallness, bright red hair, and abundant freckles, he often seemed to fade into the woodwork.

Not so Ramon. He started snapping his fingers and humming a tune. "It means the . . . 'toe bone's connected with the . . . foot bone. The foot bone's connected with the . . . ankle bone, the—' "

Jess rolled her eyes and interrupted him. "What it *means,* is that every action has a reaction. Everything you do has a consequence. And the consequences sometimes show up where you'd least expect them."

"Like, when you fall asleep with your hair wet," asked Sienna, "and when you wake up it's a rat's nest so that it gets in your eyes and you end up tripping on a chair on your way to the mirror?"

17

Cary frowned. "We're talking about the *environment*. What did Freedom mean when he said that about our trash?"

Ramon went on singing, and even got up to add a funky dance. " 'The ankle bone's connected with the . . . leg bone. The leg bone's connected with . . .' "

Ignoring him, Jess answered Cary. "Well, let's think about it. I threw away a yogurt container today. That container is going to sit in the city dump with millions more containers and trash that other people threw away. It takes decades, at least, for things to break down and decompose. Maybe centuries. The dump fills up, and we have to find land for new dumps for more trash. That land might be in a forest or a marsh or some other place where animals live. There goes their home, right?"

"I've heard that dumps cause pollution sometimes," said Webb. "Toxic wastes."

Ramon squinted. "Yeah. I saw that on TV. Even harmless-looking junk like a pudding cup can break down and turn into disgusting chemicals that seep out and get into the water supply and stuff."

"Ew, yuck! I could be drinking my pudding cup!" Sienna plunked down her glass of lemonade.

Jess shrugged. "Could be. And so could the fish and birds, if the toxic waste gets into rivers and streams."

"Wait. I think I'm beginning to get this." Cary leaned her head sideways. "Okay. I throw something away. I never see it again. But that doesn't mean that's the end of it. It doesn't just disappear."

Webb nodded. "Every action has a reaction."

"I get it," said Ramon. "Let's say that river flows into the ocean, where dolphins live. Then dolphins can

18

be hurt by the toxic waste. Something can go from your lunch sack to the dump to a river to an ocean, into a dolphin. Everything *is* connected.'' He broke into song again. ''The river is connected with the . . . ocean. The ocean's connected . . .''

Sienna's eyes widened. ''My pudding cup could be killing dolphins at this very moment.''

Jess shrugged again. ''Well, possibly.''

There was a sober silence. Even Ramon stopped singing.

Cary broke it with, ''So, what Freedom meant was that there's no point in protecting animals if they're not going to have a decent place to live.''

''None of us is going to have a decent place to live if we don't watch out.'' Ramon wagged his finger.

''That's right,'' agreed Webb. ''Everything is connected. I mean, I see how this has to do with dogs and cats, too, not just wildlife. If the environment is bad for fish and birds and deer and things, it'll end up being bad for people, too, and for our pets. We all live on the same planet, breathe the same air, drink the same water. . . .''

''I don't want to drink my pudding cup,'' said Sienna.

Ramon grimaced. ''Gross. Very gross.''

''I think Freedom had a really good idea,'' Cary said.

''You mean cutting down on our trash?'' asked Webb.

Cary nodded. ''Yeah. Sure. Plus . . .''

Jess saw the wheels turning in Cary's head. There was a certain look that appeared on her face whenever she got an idea.

Cary went on. ''Remember when Freedom asked us

19

why we care about animals if we don't care about the earth?''

"I care," replied Ramon.

"Me, too," added Sienna.

Webb nodded.

"Maybe we need to do more than care," Jess proposed.

"Right," agreed Cary.

Jess pictured herself in a white lab coat working at a table lined with rows of test tubes and computer printouts. Next she saw herself standing in a boat on the high seas, counting humpback whales as they dove and surfaced just yards away. The scene changed to a factory next to a steamy brown river, where she filled a vial with polluted water to take back to her laboratory.

Webb's voice cut in on her daydream. "You mean, we could stretch our club's goals. Expand them."

"Do ecology stuff," Ramon put in. "Save the environment."

Jess's daydream took her away again. Dr. Jessica McCabe, scientist. Biologist, maybe. Or chemist. Or maybe both. She saw herself at a podium giving lectures and pointing at charts.

"Ecology is very hip right now," Sienna's voice broke in. "Everyone's into it."

Cary laughed. "That's true. You hear about it a lot. Even the mall shops and department stores jumped on the bandwagon last Earth Day, remember? Everything was eco-this, eco-that ..."

"Hey, I've got it!" Ramon suddenly announced. "Eco-kids!"

Everybody looked at him.

"Get it? The eco-kids!" he repeated.

"Eco-kids," Jess murmured. *"Hmm."*

Webb nodded. "I like it. If we're going to take on environmental issues, that would be a great thing to call ourselves."

"I guess we will need a new name." Cary smiled. " 'Five Cat Club' won't really cover what we're trying to do anymore."

Sienna reached down and pulled Tolkien, Cary's kitten, into her lap. "But you and your brother and sisters will still be our mascots!" she assured him, nuzzling his orange fur.

Jess thought of her own club mascot at home. Curie was named after Madame Marie Curie, the French scientist who won two Nobel prizes. Little Curie probably wouldn't notice the change in the club name, but to Jess it felt very important—like the start of something big.

How many people could a 747 jet seat? Shifting from foot to foot, Jess watched passenger after passenger come down the ramp from the airplane. She wondered when on earth her sister would be one of them. It was Sunday morning, and she and her mother, father, and grandmother had been waiting in the airport half an hour for Beth. First the plane was late, and now it seemed she might not even be on it.

"Are you sure this was her flight?" Dad asked.

Mama nodded. "Of course I'm sure. I wouldn't have made a mistake about *this*."

Jess knew it was true. The whole family had missed Beth badly over the summer while she studied at an art school in New York City, then traveled with Mama's sister Alice to Paris. It seemed that Beth's homecoming was all they talked about. Jess had set her alarm for

21

6:30 that morning so that she'd be the first one ready for the trip to the airport in nearby San Diego. She could hardly wait to see her sister. It had been three whole months!

"Well, there she is!" Grammy proclaimed.

Jess craned her neck to see above the crowd. "Where?" It was funny how Grammy in her wheelchair was always the first to spot things.

"Elizabeth!" Mama cried.

Dad ran forward into the crowd and threw his arms around a tall girl in a short white dress and red hat.

Jess blinked. That wasn't Beth, was it? The girl looked like a New York fashion model, not her fifteen-year-old sister.

After Dad's hug, Beth beelined to Mama for another, then reached down to Grammy. Normally a no-nonsense sort of person, Grammy hugged back like she'd never let go, then dabbed a hankie at her eyes. Dad's eyes were misty, too, and Mama was openly sniffling.

Finally Beth turned to Jess with her old greeting. "Hi, cutie-pie!"

Jess flung her arms around her sister.

"Oh, it's so good to see you!" Beth whispered after a long hug. "You look great."

"So do you!" Jess replied.

Beth shrugged and smiled. "Thanks. It's good to be home."

In the car on the way home Beth told them all about the trip to Paris with Aunt Alice and Cousin Janelle, for which Mama and Dad had let Beth miss the first week of tenth grade.

"It's a city of art," Beth said with a wistful sigh. "I've never been in a place like that before, where almost everywhere you turn there's something beautiful. Something old and historic, something *made* to be looked at. . . ."

"So it beats Jewel Beach?" Dad grinned.

Beth grinned back. "Slightly."

"What I want to hear about is the French food," Grammy told her. "What did you have to eat?"

That launched Beth into a rapturous description of a stew called *cassoulet,* and of a creamy pastry named after the Emperor Napoleon. Then she told a funny story about Aunt Alice, who had learned French in Canada, having a heated debate with a Parisian waiter over the correct pronunciation of the French word for butter.

Jess couldn't hear enough of her sister's stories. Beth had written home almost every week while she was away, but it just wasn't the same. And Beth had changed so much over the summer! The two of them still looked like sisters—same dark skin, chocolate brown eyes, strong chins. Beth, though, had grown up. Not only was she several inches beyond Jess's medium height, but she seemed far beyond their three-year age difference, too.

Arriving home, Dad and Jess helped carry three bulging suitcases into Beth's room. There Jess plopped down on the bed to watch her sister unpack. That was where she always sat to talk with Beth about everything under the sun.

Beth carried a stack of T-shirts to her dresser.

"You need any help?" Jess asked.

Her sister shook her head. "No, thanks."

Leaning back against the pillows, Jess slipped her hands behind her head. "When do we get to see your prize-winning paintings?"

Beth smiled. "They're not prize-winning. They were

23

just in a show. Some of us were selected to have our work shown. The big deal was that it was at the Highlight Gallery. It's a part of New York City called SoHo, and it's very hot.''

''Hot? As in popular?''

''Better than popular,'' Beth answered. ''Important. Very important. Anybody who's somebody gets shown at the Highlight.''

''Gosh. So now you're somebody.'' Jess smiled.

Beth laughed. ''Hardly. It takes a lot more than that to be a somebody. This is just something the gallery owner does every year for young painters from local art schools. You know, showcasing new talent.''

''Did they keep your paintings? Will we ever see them?''

''They kept them. The idea is, if I'm very lucky, for them to sell the paintings for me. But I've got some photos.''

They spent the next few minutes looking at photographs of some very odd paintings. One was splotches of color over rectangles and squares. Another was of a dog. No, not a dog. Maybe a giraffe, Jess decided.

''It's a lighting bolt in a storm,'' Beth told her. She went on to explain that her style had changed over the summer. It was no longer representational, or realistic. Now she was painting in the abstract style, like Pablo Picasso or somebody named Georges Braque.

Nodding, Jess tried to understand what it must be like to be an artist. To see a lightning bolt in your head and have it come out looking like a dog or a giraffe, and have it shown and maybe even sold in a ''hot'' gallery. Jess herself couldn't draw a decent stick figure if her life depended on it. Her own talents had always been

24

in school subjects—math and science, in particular—and in playing games like chess.

Beth was good in school, too, but her real interest had always been art. She drew and painted beautifully, even her first preschool doodles. Jess felt proud of her big sister.

"I think you're going to be famous one day," she told her.

"Do you? Thanks." Beth confessed that while strolling through Paris museums with Aunt Alice and Janelle she had imagined her own work on the walls instead of Rembrandt's or van Gogh's. She told Jess about her dream of going to college in Paris, an idea she hadn't broken to Mama or Dad yet.

Jess swore to secrecy, then began, "I had an interesting summer, too. My friends and I started up a club." She had only gotten out a couple more sentences before Beth interrupted her.

"Excuse me, Jess. That sounds interesting. But would you mind if I took some time to myself?"

"What do you mean?"

"I mean, right now. I'd like to be alone for a while." Beth hung a dress in her closet.

"Oh. Oh, sure." Jess nodded. "You must be tired." Beth nodded back.

"Sure. Well, all right," Jess agreed. "Just let me know when you want company. I'm really glad you're home." She headed for the door.

Beth waved her off with a smile, then shut the door softly behind her.

Slipping her hands into her pants pockets, Jess padded down the hall toward her own room. A meow made her turn around. Curie looked up at her, tail high, requesting attention. Jess scooped her up and settled into her armchair with the latest issue of *Nature* magazine.

It was disappointing not to get to spend more time with Beth after all those months apart, but there would be time to catch up later. The long flight from New York must have been exhausting.

Jess had read only a couple of paragraphs of an article about bats when she heard the door to her sister's room open. She started to get up, then heard Beth pick up the hall telephone.

"Annette? Hi!" Beth said into the phone. "Yes, I'm home! Can you believe it? Okay. Yeah. Come right over!"

Jess frowned. Hadn't Beth just said she wanted to be alone? Having her friend Annette over for a visit hardly classified as being alone.

She felt like pointing that fact out to Beth, but swallowed it instead. What could she say, anyway? *Don't talk to Annette, talk to me.*

Jess sighed, picked up the bat article again, and scratched Curie's tummy.

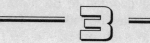

In the school cafeteria on Monday, Sienna marched up to Freedom Sutter and announced, "You can't come down on us anymore for not caring about the earth."

"Oh? Why not?" Freedom adjusted the blue bandanna he wore around his head. "Are you cleaning up your act?"

Jess and Cary held up empty soda cans.

"We're taking our cans home to Cary's brother for recycling," Jess said.

Sienna opened her lunch sack and let Freedom inspect it. Then she tossed it into one of the garbage bins nearby. "See? I didn't bring anything I didn't eat. And no pudding cup. Plus I would have reused the bag except I spilled juice in it."

"Plus," added Cary, "we're sort of changing our club."

"The Eco-kids!" cried Sienna. "Isn't that a great new name?"

Freedom crossed his arms. "So what?"

"We're expanding our focus," Jess explained, "to look not only at animals but at their habitat, too—planet Earth."

Still looking skeptical, Freedom asked, "All because of what I said to you on Friday?"

Cary shrugged. "It got us thinking."

"You mean you're changing your whole club 'cause of what I said?" His blue eyes widened in amazement.

"We're not changing our whole club," Sienna explained. "We've just decided to do more."

"Wow. Really?" asked Freedom. "Like what?"

The girls looked at each other.

"We don't know yet," Cary confessed. "So far we talked about the trash problem and recycling and cleaning up our own acts, like you said."

"Oh." Freedom shrugged.

"Don't look so dull about it," Jess told him. "At least it's a start."

"Yeah," put in Sienna. "Anyway, what are *you* doing to save the planet?"

Again, Freedom shrugged. "Mostly I try to *not* do things. Like I don't make a lot of trash, and I don't throw away things that I can use again. I try not to waste other things, either, like electricity. When I leave a room I turn the lights out. I don't let the water run while I'm brushing my teeth, and I don't—Hey!"

A red cola can whizzed right past Freedom's nose into the trash.

"Who did that?" Cary demanded.

Jess looked around at the other kids hurrying to and from the trash bins and found no likely suspects.

"Ramon!" Sienna yelled.

Turning, Jess saw that he was standing behind her with his friend Gerald.

Ramon shook his head. "Don't look at *me*. I'm innocent."

"Ha!" Sienna scoffed. "So was Benedict Arnold."

28

But Gerald had a smug look on his face. "Aw, chill out. It didn't hit ya, did it, Sutter?"

Freedom squinted at him.

"Why don't you take that can home and recycle it?" Sienna demanded.

"Huh? Carry this thing around? What a pain. No way." Gerald waved and walked off.

"Some people will never recycle." Ramon pointed at his friend. "Too much trouble." He held up his own soda can. "So what good will it do if just a few of us recycle? There'll still be millions and billions of cans in the dumps."

"Every little bit helps," said Cary.

Sienna frowned. "I don't know. Ramon has a point. It feels like a waste of time when it's only helping a *little*." She sighed, discouraged. "And it *is* a pain to carry the cans home."

Jess watched as more aluminum cans, along with food and wrappings of all sorts flew past them into the garbage. She counted three whole apples, seven soda cans, and two recyclable plastic soda bottles.

"Gerald Heimler is never going to recycle," Ramon repeated, "not if he has to work at it. Maybe if it was easier . . ."

"You mean if he didn't have to carry the can around?" suggested Cary.

"Yes." Jess nodded. "Maybe if . . ."

"Right here." Freedom pointed at the trash bins. "What if Gerald didn't have to carry it any farther than right here?"

They all looked at the bins. Then they all looked at each other.

* * *

29

"You want to start a *what?*" asked Mr. Montoya, frowning from under bushy black eyebrows.

"A recycling center," Cary repeated, "here at school."

"In the cafeteria," added Freedom, "where everyone throws their trash away. We could set up recycling bins instead."

Mr. Montoya stroked his whiskery cheeks with a thumb and forefinger. He was everybody's favorite science teacher. Jess liked him because he answered her questions seriously and encouraged her to ask more. Other kids liked Mr. Montoya because he was sarcastic—even about other teachers and the principal—and because he treated students mostly like adults. He called them Ms. McCabe and Mr. Warcheski and Ms. Phan. But Mr. Montoya could be a bear if you crossed him, threatening you with those frowning eyebrows, unshaven cheeks, and sharp black eyes.

"A recycling center." He leaned back in his desk chair until it lifted off its front legs. The back of his balding head rested against the blackboard.

It had been Freedom's idea to talk to the teacher about their new plan. On the first day of school Mr. Montoya had told the class he would discuss ecology and environmental issues throughout the year and that students could earn extra credit by bringing in newspaper articles on the subject.

"He's bound to be interested," Freedom had said. "Let's go see him."

They had marched off together—Jess, Cary, Ramon, and Freedom—all except Sienna, who had to go to a drama club meeting. Just minutes before fifth period, they found Mr. Montoya in his classroom, the science lab, grading quizzes and munching on potato chips, even though food was forbidden in Jewel Beach Junior High classrooms.

"Hmm," he said, stroking chip crumbs off his whiskers. "You people actually want to do this yourselves? You're not just proposing it as a brilliant idea that you want someone else to put together for you?"

"We're a club," said Ramon. "We do a lot of things ourselves."

"Oh." Mr. Montoya pushed his lips out and nodded.

"We're the Eco-kids," Cary filled in. "We were the Five Cat Club over the summer, working on animal problems, and now we're . . ."

"Branching out," provided Jess, "into environmental issues. We see the problem here at school as our first challenge."

"The problem?" repeated Mr. Montoya. "Meaning?"

"Lots of recyclable things are thrown away every day here," Freedom answered, his voice high-pitched with amazement that Mr. Montoya didn't know. "Haven't you noticed?"

Mr. Montoya shrugged. "Now that you mention it, yes. Even in the teacher's lounge, all those soft drink cans end up in the trash."

"Some plastics are recyclable, too," said Jess.

"Like drink bottles, right?" asked Ramon, turning to Freedom.

He nodded. "We'd set up a different bin for each type of thing—aluminum cans, plastics, glass—and people would only have to toss them in the right one. Just like the bins they have in grocery store parking lots."

Mr. Montoya nodded and let his chair fall back to all four legs with a thud. "Terrific. Then what?"

31

"Huh?" asked Cary.

"So everybody chucks the trash into the appropriate bins. Great. But that's not the happy ending, is it? Where does the stuff go from there?"

Jess looked at Freedom. Personally, she hadn't thought past the bins. Maybe he had.

"That's why we've come to you," Freedom answered. "We thought you'd have some suggestions on how to do this."

Mr. Montoya stood up and stretched. "Do you folks happen to know anything about how things work around here?"

"Around where?" asked Roman. "School?"

"Exactly," replied the teacher. "There is such a thing as a chain of command. I am not at the top of it. Neither, of course, are you. As appealing and as worthwhile as your idea sounds, you won't budge one inch with it unless you get an okay from the head banana."

"The principal?" asked Cary. "Mr. Gormley?"

"The very same. Without his stamp of approval you might as well hang it up. And getting that approval—" Mr. Montoya erased the blackboard in preparation for his next class. "Well, let's just say you could try to squeeze water from a stone."

Jess's heart sank. Why did adults make things so complicated?

"However—" Mr. Montoya dusted his hands off on his faded gray trousers. "I happen to enjoy putting the squeeze on stones. I also happen to think your idea is a very good one."

"Then you'll help us?" asked Ramon.

"You'll need an ally when you go in to talk with Mr. Gormley. 'Faculty sponsor' is the official term."

The students for his next class started coming in.

"So," said Mr. Montoya, "we'll see how far we go."

Friday afternoon, Jess's mother sat at the kitchen table poring over the account books for the charity she worked on. Jess's sister stood at the sink, trying to scrub a chocolate stain out of her new silk blouse. Only Grammy seemed to be paying any attention at all to Jess.

"The principal had the most suspicious look on his face," she was saying. "As if we had asked him to let us start up a cocktail lounge, not a recycling center!"

"How did you convince him?" Grammy looked up from the bowl of peas she was shelling.

"Oh, Mr. Montoya vouched for us. He told Gormley that we had come up with the idea ourselves and that we're a 'committed bunch of young people.' Mr. Gormley likes hearing things like that. But he asked us about a million questions. It felt like a courtroom. Plus he made us promise it wouldn't cost the school a cent to start recycling. He gave us a long lecture about the school district's budget crisis and everything. How they're nearly broke as it is."

Beth didn't seem to have heard a word.

"Beth, does Mar Vista High have recycling?" Jess asked.

"Hmm?"

For all the attention Beth paid Jess these days, she felt like a flea in her big sister's ear. "I said, do you recycle at your school?"

"Recycle? No." Beth didn't look up from her blouse.

And Mama never looked up from her paperwork, either. She had on her thick glasses, the gold hoop earrings that set off her dark skin so prettily, and her old pink sweater. Her black hair was pulled into its smooth, familiar bun on top of her head. Altogether a very familiar picture of Mama. But she might as well have been a stranger to Jess or not even there.

"Well," said Grammy, "when does your club get started?"

"We have a lot of work to do before we can even get started." Jess popped a few peas into her mouth and watched Curie scurry across the floor after one that Grammy had dropped. "We have to figure out things like . . . what, exactly, is recyclable and who will haul it away for us after we collect it—all kinds of stuff. Freedom Sutter is checking with his mother on what she knows about recycling, because they have a program at the clinic where she works. And Mr. Montoya said he'd ask around, too. Meanwhile, the rest of us are meeting at Cary's tomorrow to talk about what more we can all do."

Grammy nodded. "Sounds like teamwork."

Grammy hardly ever gave direct compliments to anyone but Curie. But Jess saw that her brown eyes and broad face, both the rich, smooth color of oak bark, shone with pride.

At least someone in this house was still interested in what Jess had to say.

"Sienna, please hurry," Cary called.

She and Jess waited at the cafeteria door while Sienna chatted with her new friends from the drama group.

It was Wednesday, the day of an important meeting scheduled with Mr. Montoya to go over the information they had all gathered during the past week.

34

Having rushed through her cheese sandwich to be on time for the 12:30 meeting, Jess was in no mood to wait for anybody.

She tugged on Cary's sleeve. "Let's just go. She'll take forever."

Cary sighed. "Good-bye, Sienna!"

As they started to walk away someone stopped them.

"Cary! Jess!" The blond girl—the one who always sat in front of Cary in English class—was out of breath.

"Oh, hi, Vivian," Cary greeted her.

"*Phew!* I ran to catch you. I've been wondering . . ." Vivian pushed her aviator-style glasses into place. "Your club? The animals club? It sounded really great when you told us about it in class. I like animals, too. Do you, um . . . ever take new members?"

Cary shrugged. "Well, it started out just three of us, and now there are five."

"No—six, counting Freedom," Jess pointed out.

Things had been happening so fast, no one had really noticed that Freedom was as active as anyone on their new project. He certainly deserved to be an Eco-kids member.

"Are you saying you'd like to join?" Jess asked.

Vivian nodded. The blue eyes behind her glasses blinked cautiously.

Cary grinned. "Come on, then. You're just in time for our meeting. We'll fill you in on the way."

In Mr. Montoya's classroom they pulled up lab stools around his desk.

"Has everyone met our new member, Vivian Rosenblatt?" he asked. "Glad you're here, Ms. Rosenblatt. Seems we finally have some concrete information to talk about today."

35

Sienna hadn't shown up yet, but Mr. Montoya always started on time no matter what. Punctuality was another thing Jess admired about him.

"'Finally' is right," said Ramon. "This has taken forever. I thought all we had to do was set up the bins and presto . . . we'd have recycling."

"I think we've all learned there's more to it than that." Mr. Montoya gave them a twisted grin. "Why don't you give us your news first, Mr. Sutter?"

Freedom nodded. "My mother volunteers on a recycling program at the health clinic where she works, and she said the first thing they had to do was figure out which parts of their garbage were recyclable. Next, they had to find someone who would come and pick it up and take it to whoever actually does the recycling. It turns out that the same company that hauls the clinic's regular trash also hauls recyclables."

"The company is Smayle Industries," Cary put in. "Freedom passed all that information on to me, and guess what I found out." She grinned. "Smayle picks up our school's garbage, too. Isn't that great? We're in business!"

"What do you mean?" asked Vivian. "We're ready to start the program?"

"Not quite," Cary confessed. "But I called Smayle and they said they provide free recycling pickup service to schools and hospitals. All we have to do is collect the recyclable stuff in big bins that they'll give us, and they'll come pick it up on a regular schedule."

"Wow," said Ramon. "So what more do we need?"

Freedom shook his head. "Not much. According to my mother one of the hardest parts about setting up a

36

program is lining up that 'vendor'—the company to pick up and handle your recyclables."

"Super," commented Mr. Montoya. "Now what's your news, Ms. McCabe?"

"Well, after Cary told me what she'd found out, I called Smayle, too, and asked them what kinds of trash they accept for recycling. They sent me this." Jess held a printed list with photo illustrations of newspapers, brown and green glass, aluminum cans, tin cans, white paper, computer paper, and even cardboard. "The woman I talked with at Smayle said we could collect any or all of these. But she suggested we pick one or two materials for starters, to keep things simple until we figure out a good system. Plus, she said she could come out to give us some tips."

"Really?" asked Ramon. "Garbage tips?"

Jess nodded. "She called it an 'audit.' A garbage audit. She calls herself a 'garbage sniffer.' "

Vivian giggled.

"She'll take a look at a day's sample of our school's garbage," Jess explained, "and let us know what we're getting into, so to speak. I set up an appointment with her for next Tuesday afternoon."

Mr. Montoya nodded. "Good. So let's see what we've got so far. Will someone take notes on this? Number one, we've got a vendor—a company to handle the recyclables we collect."

"Number one, vendor," Vivian repeated, jotting it down in her notebook.

"Number two," Cary added, "we know what kind of recyclables they'll take."

Jess showed Vivian the list to copy from.

"Aluminum cans . . ." Vivian mumbled as she wrote.

37

Freedom leaned forward. "Number three, we have an appointment for a garbage audit."

"Garbage sniffer . . . appointment." Vivian nodded. "Tuesday, three P.M."

"I've got something more," Ramon announced.

"Number four," began Vivian.

Ramon stood up and unfolded a wrinkly sheet of notebook paper. "This is a map of the school drawn by Mr. Rinehart, the custodian. I talked with him yesterday, and he said this is where the big garbage bins are, and this is where it's all picked up from." Ramon flicked his finger at various spots on the map. "But here's the most important thing he said. Listen to this. Mr. Rinehart said that he heard from a maintenance man at a company downtown that recycling actually *saves* them money. They don't have to pay the trash haulers as much 'cause there's less trash to haul."

"Really?" Cary clapped her hands.

"Hmm." Jess nodded. "That makes sense."

"And maybe it would make Mr. Gormley happy," Freedom suggested.

"Mr. Gormley the principal?" asked Vivian. "What is he unhappy about? Doesn't everyone like recycling?"

Mr. Montoya shrugged. "School budgets are stretched tighter than drums these days. Mr. Gormley and every other principal in this district—maybe the whole state—is struggling just for enough money to operate the school."

"So"—Freedom squinted thoughtfully—"if we could save him some money, we could go a long way with this project."

Mr. Montoya nodded. "You Eco-kids could go a very long way with this project. And I think you will."

"Amazing. You showed up." Jess raised her eyebrows at Sienna, who responded with an upward turn of her nose.

"Yeah, Sienna," said Cary. "You've missed all our meetings lately. Why show for this?"

Sienna waved her hand backward as if shooing away a fly. "Lay off, you two. I've been busy. And I wanted to see this. See what a garbage sniffer looks like."

The three of them leaned against the brick wall at the school's main entrance, waiting for Ms. Hong, the garbage auditor from Smayle Industries.

Jess shook her head at Sienna. "You haven't done anything for the recycling project so far. We should make you sit a double shift on the pet care hot line this week." She grinned.

"Not a bad idea," Cary agreed.

Sienna gasped. "Don't you dare. I'm way too busy. And there's no law about how much time a person has to spend on club activities. I do plenty. Plus, I've got a lot else going. My drama club is *so-o-o* incredible, you guys. You've got to come watch us rehearse sometime." Her hazel eyes sparkled. "Kendra and Mandy are so much fun. Even though Kendra is in eighth grade, she's not snobby, and she was really helpful when Ms. Tartoff assigned us to a skit together. Oh, and our group is really good. The club is going to do a musical medley called 'Fairy Tale Fun' and Ms. Tartoff says . . .''

Jess tuned out. Sienna could go on forever about her drama club or whatever other thing she happened to be ''into'' that particular week. Yet she hardly ever wanted to listen to anyone else about *her* life.

The arrival of a red convertible sports car at the curb brought an end to Sienna's flow of talk. Its license plate read RE CY KL.

''Re-cy-cle,'' Cary sounded it out. ''Must be Ms. Hong.''

A slender woman in a stylish purple suit stepped out from the driver's seat carrying a leather briefcase.

''*That's* a garbage sniffer?'' Sienna whispered.

Smiling, Ms. Hong strode up the walk and shook the girls' hands. ''Hi. I'm Charlene Hong. One of you must be Jess McCabe.''

''That's me. Thank you for coming, Ms. Hong. These are other club members, Sienna Sabo and Cary Chen.''

''Hello. Good to meet you. Are you going to show me around?''

The girls nodded.

''Our faculty sponsor, Mr. Montoya, has a teachers' meeting right now,'' explained Jess, ''but he said he'll find us later. Do you want to start with the outdoor dumpsters?''

''Sure,'' Ms. Hong answered. ''How many locations are there?''

As they talked, they headed for the back of the school office building. Jess wondered how on earth elegant Ms.

Hong was going to audit the school's garbage dressed as she was.

When they reached the garbage collection area behind the administration building, Mr. Rinehart unlocked the gate and led them in.

Ms. Hong nodded toward the two huge blue dumpsters. "How frequent is your pickup with us?" she asked the custodian.

"Once a week, on Tuesdays," answered Mr. Rinehart in his German accent. He made "once" sound like "vunce" and "week" sound like "veek."

"Does most of the throwaway come from the school offices and classrooms, or from the cafeteria, or is it leaves and clippings from the school grounds?"

Mr. Rinehart leaned his gray-haired head to one side, puffing out his chubby pink cheeks. "Vell, here vee collect zee rubbish from zee classrooms and offices, from zee school grounds. Zat is no problem. But vat comes from zee cafeteria—ah!—that is like an avalanche. You can go see."

After Ms. Hong jotted a few notes on a leather-bound pad, she thanked Mr. Rinehart. Then the girls led their visitor through the sunny central courtyard that ran between the two rows of classrooms.

At the end of the courtyard they reached the cafeteria and walked around it to a little alley.

"Oh, my," said Ms. Hong.

Jess had never been in trash alley before. That's what everyone called it. Now she knew why. A mountain of paper bags, plastic bags, banana peels, soda cans, and fruit juice boxes rose up from the dumpster and spilled over the sides to the pavement below.

Ms. Hong clucked her tongue. *"Tsk-tsk."* Out of her

41

briefcase she pulled a pair of plastic gloves. "Let's take a look."

She poked into one of the mounds on the pavement, causing cans and plastic drink bottles to clatter about. Soon she had built separate little piles of aluminum cans, plastic bottles, and paper bags.

"Do you know what these are?" she asked.

"Cans, bottles, and bags," said Jess.

Cary shrugged. "Garbage."

Sienna held her nose. "Stinky."

"These," said Ms. Hong, "are gold mines."

"Oh." Sienna looked doubtful.

"And all you have to do to get that gold is what I just did." Ms. Hong pulled off her gloves and slipped them back into her briefcase. "Separate the materials. Then let my company haul it away."

"What do you mean by gold?" asked Cary.

"The usual thing." Ms. Hong shrugged. "Money. You collect the recyclables, and we'll pay you for them."

Jess frowned. "You mean, since you won't be hauling away just worthless garbage anymore, it will reduce the school's hauling bill?"

Ms Hong shook her head. "No. Well, I mean, yes. We can reduce the school's hauling bill if we're collecting less throwaway material. But that's not all. We will actually pay you for the recycled materials you separate for us."

"Pay us? Money?" Sienna's eyes doubled in size.

Ms. Hong laughed. "Certainly you've heard of collecting recyclables for cash. Don't you ever see people doing that—combing through trash bins for cans and glass? They bring them to us and we pay them. We, in

42

turn, are paid by the manufacturer that performs the actual recycling process, transforming the soda cans into fresh aluminum cans or whatever.''

"Gosh," said Cary. "We never thought about that."

Ms. Hong smiled. "Let me warn you, though. I'm not talking about an enormous amount of money. If you want to know the truth, my advice is don't get hung up on the money aspect. I mean, no one should start a recycling program for the money alone. Recycling for a big organization like this—a school, a business, whatever—requires a lot of work and commitment. It's never a piece of cake. You've got to have other reasons to keep you going.''

Jess shrugged. "We do have other reasons. We didn't even know we could make money when we decided to recycle. It's for our club, the Eco-kids.''

"The environment," added Cary. "We want to do our share to keep it clean.''

"And to help animals," Sienna chimed in. "I don't want my pudding cup to poison dolphins.''

Ms. Hong smiled. "Well, sounds like you have your goals in place. Now, why don't we go sit down somewhere, and I'll give you a few ideas on how to get started.''

Jess led the way to Mr. Montoya's classroom, thinking about the things Ms. Hong had said. She had a good point about recycling for the right reasons. All the same, Jess wondered just how much "gold" there might be in that dumpster.

"I still think we should have gone for the whole thing." Arms crossed, Freedom aimed a disgruntled frown at a cardboard box labeled CANS. Decorated with

43

Vivian's illustrations of different brands of sodas, it sat in the cafeteria trash alcove next to the garbage bins where Ramon had just placed it. "We should collect everything—cans, plastic bottles and paper sacks here in the cafeteria. White paper and computer paper in the school offices and classrooms. Cardboard, glass—"

Jess interrupted him with a shake of her head. "I disagree. Ms. Hong suggested we start our program with just one material."

"That's right," echoed Cary. "Keep it simple till we get our system going."

"All I ever hear these days is Ms. Hong said this and Ms. Hong said that," Ramon complained. "We don't have to do whatever she says."

Vivian shrugged. "Well, she knows what usually works, right? She's helped other groups start recycling. But maybe Freedom is right about our being able to handle more than just cans."

"Well, no matter who's right or wrong, this is what we've got for today." Ramon waved at the box. "So let's just shut up, go eat our lunches, and see what happens, okay?"

Everyone nodded and took his advice.

Sienna wandered over just as the girls arrived at their table. "Hi. What's up? Any contributions yet?" She peered back at the box. "Cute sign, Vivian."

"Thanks. But there's nothing there except for the samples we put in."

After finishing lunch, Sienna held up her strawberry soda can like a trophy. "Well, here's my first contribution."

"And here's mine," added Jess, draining the last swallow from her cola.

44

The two of them marched toward the bins with Cary and Vivian following.

"This is funny," noted Vivian. "We must look like an army."

Cary nodded. "Let's us soldiers go see what happened during lunch."

What had happened, they soon saw, was nothing. The box contained the same three cans as before, and nothing more.

"This is terrible," mumbled Vivian.

"Hey!" Sienna pointed at a boy tossing away his lunch sack. "Got an aluminum can in there?"

"In here?" He shook his head. "No. But my sister probably does."

The boy pointed at an older girl approaching from the other side. She carried a green can which she started to toss into the garbage.

"Stop!" cried Sienna.

The girl's head jerked up in surprise. "Who? Me?"

"Why are you throwing that away?" asked Jess.

"This?" The girl frowned at the can, puzzled. "Because it's trash."

"Why not put in the box?" asked Cary.

Vivian pointed at the CANS sign.

"Well, okay. But how come? Why do you want it?"

"Recycling," said Sienna, "to save the dolphins."

The girl looked even more puzzled, but dropped her can in the box anyhow.

"Thank you," Jess told her.

"You're welcome," answered the girl, backing away as if she were dealing with lunatics.

Jess sighed. "I think we're going to have to try a new approach."

45

Vivian nodded. "Definitely."

The boys walked over from their table.

"Well, how's it going?" Ramon asked cheerily. Then he saw the nearly empty box.

"Oh," said Freedom.

"Has anyone here ever heard of the four R's?" Cary asked. She leaned against a corner of the teacher's desk in an eighth grade math class.

Jess sat on the other corner, feeling more nervous than ever before. Twenty-nine eighth graders stared at her and Cary, some looking terminally bored, and others with the same "You're crazy" look that the girl had given them in the cafeteria. Why, Jess was starting to wonder, had she agreed to do this?

When none of the students responded to Cary's question, Mr. Beale volunteered, "Reading, 'riting, 'rithmetic and . . . ?"

"That's the *three* R's," a boy in the second row pointed out.

"That's right," Cary agreed. "The *four* R's are for . . ."

Just as they'd practiced earlier, Jess held up a big sign that Vivian had drawn up on poster board. Underneath a green letter *R* it read,

RETHINK, REDUCE, REUSE, RECYCLE

Mr. Montoya had helped them come up with the slogan during a brainstorming session.

The few faces that glanced up at the poster looked

blank to Jess. Other students doodled in their notebooks, passed notes, or tossed erasers at each other. Jess felt like a fool trying to get her schoolmates to listen. But that's what the Eco-kids had decided to do—go out in teams to all the classrooms and tell Jewel Beach Junior High students about the recycling program. Otherwise it would never get off the ground.

"*R* is for 'rethink,' " said Cary, "because we have to rethink the way we do things."

"For instance . . ." Jess scanned the room. She spotted Oliver Camstock, who played forward for the Jewel Beach Royals basketball team. She took a breath, gathering courage. "Oliver, how much do you weigh?"

"Huh?" He shrugged. "Hundred and eight."

"Thank you. Well, imagine this," Jess began. "Oliver's family and everyone else's in this whole room, even in this whole United States, produces almost enough garbage to match Oliver's weight every week."

"Every *week?*" repeated Mr. Beale.

Cary nodded. "An average of one hundred pounds per week per household."

Jess saw someone yawn.

"That's one hundred sixty million tons of trash per year that we produce in our country *alone*," she said, thinking that might drive the point home.

No one even blinked.

"One hundred sixty million tons," Cary repeated. "If you loaded that onto garbage trucks and lined them up bumper to bumper . . ."

Jess held up the next poster, on which Vivian had drawn a convoy of garbage trucks riding through outer space.

"They would reach halfway to the moon!" Cary declared.

Some of the faces in the classroom perked up. Jess saw a few students actually studying the poster.

"Yuck," one of them said.

"What a bunch of garbage!" guffawed a boy in the back, inspiring gales of laughter.

"All right, keep it down," the teacher warned.

Cary shrugged. "It's okay. It *is* a bunch of garbage. A big bunch. And we're running out of places to dump it."

"Really rotten, huh?" Jess chuckled, unable to resist the pun.

"What a couple of clowns," the boy in the back called out.

"So . . . what are we going to do about it?" Cary asked.

Jess held up the *R* sign again.

"*R* is for 'reduce,' " said Cary. "Reduce what you produce."

"For instance," Jess suggested, "instead of bringing your juice for lunch in those juice boxes, you could use a thermos."

"When you're out shopping with your parents," said Cary, "try to buy stuff with less packaging. Why does a hairbrush really have to come wrapped in two layers of plastic *and* cardboard? And some stores sell foods in bulk, like breakfast cereal and peanut butter, so you can take your own container and fill it up again and again, instead of buying dozens of packages to throw away."

"Reducing the package reduces the price, too," added Jess. "You can pay less by buying smart. About one dollar out of every ten we spend on food goes for what the food is *wrapped* in, not the food itself. You

48

just throw the wrapping away. You might as well throw away a dollar bill.''

"Reduce," Cary emphasized. Then she pointed at the third *R.* "Then there's number three, reuse. Why not bring your lunch in a reusable lunch box instead of a throwaway bag?''

Jess followed with, "Before you throw anything away, *rethink.* Ask yourself, can I *reuse* this for anything? Maybe the empty strawberry baskets would be good for a school project. Or maybe a charity group could fix that wobbly old chair your dad is throwing out.''

"If you can't reuse it"—Cary pointed at the fourth *R*—"can you *recycle* it?''

Jess flipped up a new poster. Vivian's cute drawings of soda cans, glass bottles, plastic milk jugs, and stacks of newspapers scurried across the page away from a smelly-looking garbage dump. They had little ears and whiskers and worried eyes like mice escaping the clutches of a cat.

The kids laughed.

"All of these items are recyclable,'' Jess said. "That means that they can be gathered up, crushed, melted down, and turned into fresh cans or bottles or newspapers, or into something completely different.''

"Something different?'' asked a girl in front. "Like what? What can you turn plastic into?''

"You know those big plastic drink bottles?'' Cary held her hands apart to show the size. "They can make egg cartons out of those. They can even make jackets.''

"Jackets to wear?'' a boy near the front asked. "Out of plastic bottles?''

Cary nodded. "It's neat to think about it. Something you thought was garbage being made into something new.''

"Who does that?" asked the boy.

"There are factories where it's done," Jess answered. "Our local garbage company picks up our recyclables and delivers them to the manufacturing companies."

"It's that easy?" asked the girl. "We just give it to them?"

"That's all you do," Jess confirmed, feeling relieved. Finally, people seemed to be catching on.

"How many of you have noticed a new box in the cafeteria this week?" Cary asked.

Five or six hands went up.

Cary and Jess exchanged glances.

"Well . . ." Cary cleared her throat. "That box . . . See, our club, the Eco-kids . . . We're trying to start a recycling program for this school."

"For aluminum cans only right now," Jess put in. "It's really easy. All you have to do is drop your drink cans into that box."

"And we'll do the rest," said Cary, twiddling her thumbs nervously. "And you'll be helping the environment."

Jess scanned the kids' faces. The club's whole plan depended on their schoolmates. If people didn't contribute their cans, there would be nothing to recycle.

Mr. Beale turned to his students. "Well? Will you all cooperate?"

"I will," replied the boy in front.

A few others nodded.

The boy in back called out, "I *can* give you my *can*."

Mr. Beale rolled his eyes. "Very good, Richard."

Looking over the rest of the students, Jess found them still doodling, whispering, and throwing things. It was impossible to predict whether they'd cooperate or not.

50

A heavy fog shrouded Opal Street. From her doorway, Jess could barely see Cary's house across the street. Dark and misty gray, the weather fit her mood. She pulled up the hood of her jacket, tucked Curie under an arm, and started down the front path. October was supposed to be one of Jewel Beach's best months—sunny and warm—real California weather. It had always been that way before. But this fall a warm ocean current called El Niño had changed the normal climate patterns, according to an article Dad read aloud from the paper that morning.

Nothing was predictable these days. Not even Jess's own mother. Today she and Jess were supposed to go to San Diego. She had promised to take Jess to a new bookstore. Instead, an early-morning call from St. Joan's Shelter for Women, the charity Mama worked for, had caused her to hurry out there instead.

And Beth. In the old days, before Beth's summer in new York, the two of them would spend Saturday mornings making French toast. Today all Beth wanted was a roll and coffee, and that she took up to her room.

On the sidewalk in front of Cary's, Jess switched

Curie to her other arm and stopped to tie her shoelace. The kitten let out a complaining meow.

"Be patient," Jess told her. "We're going to visit your brother at Cary's."

Muffled voices drifted from across the street. Through the fog Jess made out the figures of two girls walking past her own house. One of them had long, curly hair.

"Sienna?" Jess called.

"Yes?" a voice answered.

"It's me. We're having a kitten play day at Cary's. Want to bring Number One?" Jess had always felt that that was a strange name for a cat, but . . . leave it to Sienna.

She heard a few low-spoken words she couldn't make out, and then Sienna said, "No. I'm spending the day with Mandy."

"Hi, Jess," said Mandy.

"Hi, Mandy."

"Mandy isn't into animal and environmental stuff," Sienna said. "Thanks, anyway."

Jess didn't know what to say. *Environmental and animal stuff?* What was that supposed to mean?

She rang the Chens' doorbell. Within minutes of entering Cary's house, Jess forgot about Sienna's snub, Mama's breaking her promise, and Beth holing up in her room. Being at Cary's kept a person too busy to think about much else. As usual, it was a madhouse. Buck and his friends played loud music and tramped back and forth to the kitchen for food and drink. Luke and his friends chased after one another or the dogs or Luke's hamster, which had gotten loose. Once in a while Cary's mother came out from the den to call, in vain, for quiet.

Cary and Jess retreated upstairs to Cary's room to watch the kittens play.

After Curie and Tolkien had toppled Cary's desk lamp and shredded a catnip mouse, Cary showed Jess a box from the animal shelter. "Would you help me open this? It's the pamphlets Ms. Engel sent us."

" 'Adopting a Cat.' 'Housetraining Your Puppy.' 'Spay/Neuter Saves Lives,' " Jess read. "Excellent."

Cary nodded. "They'll save us so much time. Instead of having to answer the same old questions on the pet care hot line all the time, we can just send them the right pamphlet."

"You know what could save us even more time?" Jess tapped a finger on her chin. "Let's sort them according to topic and what type of typical questions each pamphlet might answer. For example, 'Housetraining Your Puppy.' We get dozens of calls about that. Like, 'how long will it take? Should I train him on newspaper or take him outside?' And then there are the calls about whether to adopt a kitten or an adult cat. So we list all the different questions in one column." Jess pulled out her pocket notebook and started writing. "Like this. And in the column opposite we write the name of the pamphlet. Like this. So all you have to do is glance at the list to figure out which pamphlet to send out."

"Good idea," Cary agreed. "You're always great at organizing things."

Jess beamed. "Thanks. I like efficiency."

"And I'm glad you're willing to put some extra effort into the Eco-kids," Cary went on. "That's the kind of thing we need more of, or I'm afraid the recycling program will fizzle out."

53

"We've made a good try," Jess said. "We can't force people to participate."

Cary sighed. Her dark eyes gazed toward the kittens but seemed not to see them. "We're just not doing enough, you know? Our old Five Cat Club projects have gotten kind of ho-hum, too. We're not really much of a club anymore."

"What? You must be joking. We've been doing a lot."

"But we're somehow ... somehow missing our goals," Cary countered.

Jess frowned. Cary wasn't making any sense. The Five Cat Club and the Eco-kids had kept Jess very busy. Just because they hadn't changed the world yet ...

"I think we're not using all our talents," Cary went on. "Sienna, for instance. She'd have been great doing those classroom talks, much better than you or me or Ramon or Freedom."

Jess agreed with that. "But she was too busy. She's too busy for us, period. I saw her on the way here, walking by with Mandy Sykes. You know what she said to me?"

Cary shook her head. "I probably don't want to know."

"They couldn't come over here because Mandy isn't into environmental and animal stuff." Jess snorted. "I mean, as if we're fanatics or something."

Cary rolled her eyes. "We need to change that attitude."

Glowering, Jess mulled over the fact that she had been snubbed not once but three times that morning—by her mother, her sister, and her friend! It stung. She wanted to tell Cary about it. Sometimes talking with a

54

friend helped, even though it might feel embarrassing at first. But one look at Cary changed her mind. Cary had that far-off gaze again, as if she were thinking about something else.

The doorbell rang.

"Oh, that might be Webb," said Cary. "He's bringing his kitten. Want to help me carry the pamphlets to the kitchen?"

Arms loaded, they met Webb, his little sister, Molly, and Tux at the front door.

"May I play with the kittens?" asked Molly.

"Sure," Cary replied. "Take Tux up to my room while your brother helps us set up these hot line pamphlets."

Molly raced upstairs.

In the kitchen, it turned out there really wasn't anywhere to set up the pamphlets. During the hot-line hours on weekdays, whoever was on duty sat at the table with the big red notebook full of tips on pet care problems. Between shifts, the notebook was kept in the cabinet next to the refrigerator, along with telephone books, a mound of brown paper grocery bags, an ancient electric mixer, and several bags and cans of pet food. Cary searched through all the drawers and cabinets, finding not an inch of space for the pamphlets. Finally she shoved aside the flour and sugar canisters on the countertop.

"There." She dusted off her hands. "Let's put them here, where they'll be close to the phone."

No sooner had they set up a neat pile of "Housetraining Your Puppy" than Cary's mom came in from the den.

"Hello, Jess, Webb. How are you? Wait a second."

Ms. Chen pointed with her pencil at the countertop. "What are those?"

"Pamphlets," Cary answered simply, "for the hot line."

Her mother used the pencil to scratch the back of her neck. Short and slender, wearing a roomy blue sweat suit, she wore her black hair pulled into a spiky ponytail atop her head. "This is not going to work."

"Oh," said Cary.

"We're crowded enough in here as it is. There's a serious lack of counter space."

"But there's nowhere else—" Cary began.

"My point exactly," countered her mother briskly. "If there were somewhere else, it would already be filled with proper kitchen things. You need different headquarters."

Jess bit her lip. Was Ms. Chen kicking the Eco-kids out? Maybe her mom would let the club move in, but the McCabes' house wasn't much bigger than the Chens'.

"New headquarters?" Cary repeated. "Like where?"

"Well, I've been thinking." Ms. Chen stuck the pencil through her ponytail. "You've more members now, and it's dreadfully crowded for all of us when you hold your meetings. Sometimes we have to bounce you out of the kitchen to the den, don't we? It's utter chaos. And of course I realize your bedroom is much too small for meetings, so"—she walked toward the door leading to the garage—"how about . . . ?"

"The garage?" Cary's eyes brightened. "Mom, what a terrific idea! A headquarters. That's just what we need. That's what I was talking about, Jess—something to really get us moving!"

Jess nodded while Cary's mother fit a key into the door lock. Having a real headquarters, where the club could store and organize the pamphlets and everything else, where they could meet every week in quiet and privacy, a solid home base . . . it would be great.

Ms. Chen jiggled the key back and forth until it turned. Then she shoved mightily at the door. It creaked, groaned, and gave way, but opened only a few inches before jamming against something.

"Boxes," Ms. Chen explained.

Cary poked her head through the opening. "*Lots* of boxes." She moved to let Jess and Webb see.

The garage was dark, musty, and a total mess. Jess sneezed. "Not exactly a palace." She smiled at Cary's mom.

Ms. Chen laughed. "True, but the good news is that it's all yours."

Until Sunday afternoon, Jess wasn't convinced that having something like the Chens' garage as "all theirs" was good news for the Eco-kids. The place was better suited to be a haunted house than a club headquarters.

After a few hours of cleanup, though, the idea started to seem better. Webb had come back to help on Sunday. Along with Jess, Cary, and her mom, they swept dust balls from the floor, cobwebs from the ceiling, and dragged box after box of broken toys, old magazines, and just plain junk to the curb. Delighted to have her garage cleaned out, Ms. Chen called Jess's mother to ask if St. Joan's shelter could use any of the things. They arranged a pickup for Tuesday morning.

Meanwhile, Sienna dropped by and actually helped for a while. Mostly she tried to convince Ms. Chen to hold a garage sale, to which Ms. Chen replied that she'd rather die than take anyone's money for a scorched Daffy Duck lamp shade or a dog-stained beach towel.

By Monday afternoon, the Eco-kids had more good news.

Jess came home after school calling, "Mama? Mama! You home?"

"In here, honey," her mother replied from the den.

"Guess what!" Jess bounded in and gave her an enthusiastic hug, almost toppling the pile of paperwork in Mama's lap.

Grammy wheeled in from her room next door. "I know. You made another *A* in your science class, didn't you?"

Jess shook her head. "The test isn't till Wednesday. But listen to this. So many people recycled their cans in the cafeteria today that our box overflowed!"

"Marvelous, honey!" Mama took off her glasses.

Grammy nodded. "Recycling. Well, well. Never heard of it before I came to California. But it's a good thing, isn't it? Good for the environment and all."

"Yes, Mama," Jess's mother answered her own. "This is a wonderful thing that Jess and her club are doing."

Jess beamed as her mother gave her a one-armed hug.

"I read in the paper about the world running out of resources and all," said Grammy. "I guess people my age and yours"—she pointed at her daughter—"maybe we just used too much in our time. It's you young folks who are having to clean up after us. Figure out a new way."

Jess shrugged. "Rethink, reduce, reuse, and recycle. That's what we're doing so far."

"Sounds fascinating." Beth strolled in from the

58

kitchen. She sat on the sofa and took an apple from the fruit bowl on the end table.

"It sure does." Grammy nodded.

Jess started to explain, "It's called the four *R*'s, because—"

"You've become quite the environmentalist, haven't you?" Beth interrupted, taking a bite of the apple. "You and your pals don't play jacks on the sidewalk anymore."

Jess shook her head. Actually, she and her friends had never played jacks on the sidewalk. Hopscotch and statues, maybe, but not jacks. She didn't point that out to her sister, though. It was a miracle that Beth was talking to her at all. "We're learning a lot," she said. "It's fun. We just set up a new headquarters in Cary's garage, and our school recycling program is finally taking off, so—"

"That's great," Beth interrupted again.

The stern look on Grammy's face was impossible to miss. It was aimed straight at Beth.

"Um, Jess, I was wondering . . ." Beth sighed. "You want to go to the mall?"

"The mall?" Jess repeated in disbelief. "Now?"

"Well, if you're busy, never mind—"

"She's not," Grammy interrupted sharply.

"You can do your homework after dinner," Mama put in.

"Well . . ." murmured Jess. Something fishy was going on. Beth never asked her to do things anymore. Obviously, Grammy and Mama had put her up to it. But the fact of the matter was that Jess didn't care.

"Okay," she said. It would be wonderful to spend

some time with Beth again. To talk, to laugh, to be sisters.

"Let's go." Beth looked at her watch. "Kandi's picking us up any minute."

Kandi, not one of Jess's favorites among her sister's friends, honked her car horn in front of the house just seconds later. On the way to the mall, she uttered about three words to Jess. During the hour that the three of them walked up and down past the shops and restaurants of West Beach Mall, she said nothing to Jess. Beth responded to her sister's questions and comments, but otherwise made little effort to acknowledge her existence. Jess felt like a fifth wheel, a tagalong.

In front of Wexler's department store, while Kandi and Beth made fun of a mannequin's sixties "mod" look, Jess decided to say something.

"Excuse me." She tapped on her sister's shoulder.

Kandi glanced at her.

"What?" asked Beth.

"I'd like to go home," said Jess.

Kandi smacked her gum.

"Why?" asked Beth.

"I'm not having a good time."

"What do you expect us to do, Jessie—stand on our heads to entertain you?" Kandi sneered.

"Acting like I exist would help. Talking to me once in a while would be nice. But don't bother, Kandi. It's not like you're the most fascinating conversationalist in the world."

"Jess! Don't be rude," Beth scolded.

"Me, rude?" Jess huffed. "Right."

Kandi wrinkled her nose. "I think I've had enough of your little sister for one day, Beth."

60

"The feeling is entirely mutual." Jess made a face at the older girl.

"Just a minute, Kandi. Wait here." Beth led Jess off behind a potted plant. "You should learn to behave yourself."

Jess stared back at Beth. She almost started crying, but was determined not to. "So should *you!*"

Beth sighed. "Look, I'm sorry. I know Kandi can be a jerk sometimes and I didn't mean to gang up with her against you—"

"Then why—" Jess had to bite her lip against the tears.

"You're actually a great little sister." Beth rested a hand on Jess's shoulder. "But you've got to understand something. See, Grammy asked me to bring you along today."

"Tell me something I don't know."

"You and I can't be together all the time anymore, Jess."

Jess frowned. "Who said I wanted to be?"

Beth grinned, then shrugged. "Well, you know, we used to hang out a lot. But things are different now. I'm not a kid anymore."

"Neither am I!" Jess protested.

"Sure, not a *little* kid, but . . . you're in junior high and I'm in high school. That makes a big difference."

Jess shook her head. "You weren't like this before New York."

"Maybe not." Beth shrugged again. "All I know is, you and I have different interests now. We'll always be sisters, of course. That'll never change. I wouldn't want it to. You're a great kid. You just can't expect to hang around with me."

61

A cold knot of anger formed in Jess's belly. "Fine. Who would want to, the way you act!"

Beth shrugged. It seemed to be her reaction to everything these days. "Fine. Want us to take you home?"

Jess nodded, afraid that if she tried to speak, tears would come out instead.

6

It was hard to understand how anyone could be as mean and stupid as Beth. Jess didn't even want to think about the things her sister had said or the indifferent look she'd had on her face minutes ago when she and Kandi dropped Jess off at home.

Jess would not go inside. If she did there would be questions about why she'd come home early, and Grammy would nail Beth with a lecture later. She didn't want Grammy lecturing Beth. She simply wanted Beth to dry up, flake away, go fly a kite, and/or jump in the nearest lake.

Meanwhile, she refused to cry. Not over that stuck-up, rude sister of hers. Never!

A wrenching sound came from across the street—the Chens' garage door opening.

"It works!" she heard Cary yell.

From somewhere inside the house, Ms. Chen yelled back, "Super!"

Jess crossed the street, hands in pockets.

"Hey, Jess!" Cary smiled at her. "Just the person I wanted to see. Will you help me move this table? And look! The electric door opener works now. Mom put a new battery in the remote-control box."

Cary let Jess press the button a few times to open and close the door. Then Ms. Chen came and told them to stop. "What a godawful racket! It needs oil."

"Yeah!" yelled Sienna from the kitchen. "I'm trying to talk on the phone in here. My hot-line shift, remember?"

Jess put the control down. She and Cary left the door open while they got to work. Helping set up the headquarters felt like the best medicine to Jess. Here at Cary's she'd been welcomed right away, appreciated. Maybe she'd never go home and see her ugly sister again. Just move into the Eco-kids headquarters. The girls slid an old, scarred, and dusty dining table to the center of the garage and stood back to admire it.

"After you clean that it'll be lovely," said Cary's mother, climbing a ladder to oil the door tracks.

Cary nodded. "We need a big table like this to spread our things out."

"Do the electrical outlets in here work?" asked Jess. "We're going to need more light. On cold days we might not want to leave the door open."

"They're in fine shape," Ms. Chen confirmed. "But I'm afraid I don't have any lamps to donate."

Cary shrugged. "I'll ask Ramon if his mom has any. He's coming for hot-line duty tomorrow."

"I'll ask my parents, too," promised Jess, deciding with a sigh that she probably would go home eventually.

"Ask your parents what?" Sienna had appeared at the door from the kitchen, rubbing the back of her neck.

"For a lamp," Jess explained. "We need more light in here."

"Oh, I have a lamp I'm trying to get rid of. You know—that hideous thing in my room? I hate it. Dad

64

brought me a stained-glass one from his shop to replace it. I can go get the old one now, if you want.'' She scowled, rubbing her shoulders. ''On second thought, I'll bring it tomorrow. I'm too pooped right now. The hot-line shift was crazy. Twelve calls!'' She collapsed into a green beanbag chair in a corner. Dog hair flew up all around her. ''Yuck!''

Cary giggled. ''Sorry. That used to be Lucille's favorite.''

Sienna sighed. ''Oh, I'm too tired to care. We rehearsed 'Fairy Tale Fun' this afternoon, and Benjamin Medina and I had to practice the '*Beauty and the Beast*' waltz dance about twenty times. And then I had to race home, change, and dash over here for the hot line.''

''She tried to get out of it, too,'' Cary informed Jess.

''I did not,'' Sienna protested. ''I tried to switch days with you, that's all.''

''You still owe me for the last time we switched,'' Cary reminded her.

''*Hmm.*'' Jess took out her pocket notebook. ''Actually, you owe me, too. For . . . let's see. Once in September, once in October . . .''

Sienna sighed again. ''What trusting friends.''

''Well, I'm off to start dinner,'' said Cary's mom, heading for the kitchen. ''Try to keep your caps on in here.''

''I'm too''—Sienna began, yawning—''tired not to. And tonight Mandy and I are going to Kendra's for dinner. Mandy's meeting me here any minute now.''

''She's coming here?'' Jess wondered. ''I thought she couldn't tolerate 'animal and environmental stuff.' ''

''Well, she's not going to stay.''

''Fine with me,'' snapped Jess, then felt sorry she'd

said it. Sometimes Sienna riled her. And today she was already at her limit because of Beth.

"Aren't you in a charming mood?" Sienna huffed.

In the old days, Jess recalled, Cary would have stepped between them to referee. But sometime during the summer it seemed she had started ignoring Jess's spats with Sienna. Nowadays she and Sienna were on their own.

This time she chose not to respond to Sienna's remark—just to let it drop and go on dusting off the table.

In the silence that followed, her mind wandered to the science test coming up that week, then to her scheduled shift on the recycling crew after school. With Ramon and Vivian, she would collect the cans from the cafeteria and other boxes around the school grounds, then deposit them in the special outdoor bin provided by Smayle Industries. Easy as pie. Smayle picked them up once a week. At the end of three months they would send the school a check. Depending on the number of cans collected it could end up being just a few dollars— or maybe up to a hundred! After lunch Wednesday, the club would have a meeting to discuss how the recycling program could be improved.

Just as she was about to mention her ideas on the subject to Cary and Sienna, the sudden squeal of bicycle brakes made Jess jump.

"Hi!" cried Gina Chang. She and another little girl straddled their bikes and wore enormous, friendly grins.

"You two startled us," Cary complained. "You shouldn't sneak up on people like that."

"We didn't sneak up on you." Gina blew a green gum bubble until it popped. "We rode slowly all the way up the driveway. Didn't you see us?"

"Hi, Jess. Hi, Sienna," said freckle-faced Patti Pelligrini, smiling wide enough to show her two missing front teeth.

Both girls lived two blocks down the street. They must be about seven or eight now, Jess decided. A few years ago, just after Jess and her family had moved to Opal Street, she and Cary had let the little girls join them to play hopscotch and statues. But after a while the preschoolers had gotten on their nerves. The older girls took to playing indoors to avoid the little pests. Now they were back.

"What do you want?" asked Sienna, none too sweetly.

"We were just wondering what you were doing." Gina climbed off her bike. "Looks nice in here. You cleaning up?"

Cary nodded.

"I saw you on TV," Patti mentioned shyly.

"Did you?" Sienna asked.

"During the summer." Gina nodded. "About those dolphins."

"Yes, we're famous." Sienna slipped her hands behind her head and gazed dreamily out into the sky.

"Why are you cleaning up?" asked Gina. "Want us to help?"

"No, thanks," Jess answered quickly. "We're almost finished."

"I like cleaning up." Gina grabbed one of the rags off the table. "It's fun."

"This isn't for fun," said Cary. "It's serious. We're a club."

"A club?" Patti's eyes lit up. "Really?"

Right away, Jess knew Cary had made a mistake.

67

"Oh, can we join?" Gina begged. "Please?"

It was enough to rouse Sienna from the beanbag. She got up and marched over to the younger girls. "We're already kind of full on members, okay? Why don't you go home and help your parents clean up?"

"We want to help *you*," Gina insisted.

The older girls exchanged glances.

Finally, Jess looked down at Patti and Gina. "All right. You can help us clean a little today. But just this once. We're very busy, and we can't hang around with you much." The words echoed in Jess's head. They sounded familiar. She drove the thought away and went on wiping the table.

Delighted, Gina and Patti joined in. They attacked the table with zeal.

"Hey, easy," Cary cautioned. "Just wipe off the dust, okay? We're not trying to sand it down."

"Oh, great," Sienna groaned. "Mandy will be here any minute. She'll think I belong to a kiddie club."

Cary rolled her eyes. "Oh, calm down."

Sienna peered around the edge of the garage doorway down the street. "Yikes! Here she comes." With that, she took off.

"G'bye!" called the little girls.

Sienna didn't even glance back.

"Too bad we can't hold this meeting in our new headquarters." Ramon raked a comb through his hair.

The rest of the club members perched on their usual spots on lab stools and on the corners of Mr. Montoya's desk Wednesday afternoon.

"It's terrific," confirmed Cary. "Just like a real office. Jess's father gave us an old filing cabinet. And Ramon brought over a potted plant from a garage sale.''

''A potted plant,'' repeated Sienna, who for once had managed to show up for a meeting. ''Imagine Ramon thinking of that.''

''Maybe he's turning over a new leaf,'' remarked Mr. Montoya. ''So to speak. Well, anyway, for those of us who don't live in your neighborhood, the headquarters won't be convenient, but of course, it will be quite convenient for your other projects.''

''I can ride my bike over there,'' said Freedom. ''It's only two miles from my house.''

Vivian shook her head. ''I live farther away. But my sister can drive me over sometimes.''

''Well, one good thing,'' said Sienna, ''is that using the garage will keep us from getting kicked completely out of the Chens' house.''

Jess nodded. ''Ms. Chen was getting fed up with us.''

''True,'' agreed Cary. ''But to me the headquarters is important because it can be a home base. Something to branch out from. There's so much to do. A *million* things to do . . .''

''You've been saying that all week,'' Freedom noted. ''What, exactly, are you talking about?''

''I don't really know,'' Cary admitted. ''But I know we shouldn't call ourselves the Eco-kids if all we do is recycle cans at school and talk on the pet care hot line.''

Sienna frowned. ''Why not? That sounds like a lot to me.''

''Yeah, and it's more than anyone else does!'' Ramon agreed.

Cary shook her head. ''I don't care what anyone else does or doesn't do. It's just that *I* want to do more.''

69

"All right, hold on a minute," interrupted Mr. Montoya. "We called this meeting to discuss—"

"I want to discuss money," Sienna finished for him. "How do we get more people to recycle their cans, so we can get more cash from Smayle?"

Ramon nodded enthusiastically. "Yeah!"

"That cash might not amount to very much," Jess reminded them, "and we won't even get our first check until after the Christmas holidays, so don't get too excited."

"The more we recycle," proclaimed Ramon, "the more we'll get."

"And the less trash ends up in the dump," Vivian added.

"And the better it is for the planet," said Freedom.

Ramon nodded. "*And* for everybody *on* the planet."

"Our crew collected several full boxes of cans yesterday," Jess reported. "According to the figures Ms. Hong gave us for what a school our size might produce, that's a pretty good recycling participation level."

"That means people have gotten the message, right?" Sienna asked.

Ramon shrugged. "Even Gerald Heimler chucks his can in the box, now that it's so easy. No way would he ever have carried it home."

"The good ol' SNEASY factor." Mr. Montoya leaned back in his chair.

"Huh?" Cary wrinkled her nose.

"I came across it talking to somebody at an environmental education organization up in the San Francisco area," the teacher explained. "SNEASY stands for 'it'S Not EASY enough.' It came from a booklet they're sending me about how schools can organize recycling projects.''

Vivian giggled. ''Well, looks like we've gotten past SNEASY on cans.''

''So why not start recycling other things?'' asked Freedom, tapping his fingers impatiently on Mr. Montoya's desk.

''Gosh, you two are right!'' Cary leaned forward. ''I mean, what are we waiting for? Ms. Hong said it might take a few weeks or months to work out our system, but it hasn't taken that long. Things are going pretty well.''

Sienna groaned, then intoned in a deep voice, ''Just when you thought it was safe . . .''

Jess rolled her eyes. ''A little extra work won't kill you.''

''Like how much extra work?'' asked Ramon. ''If SNEASY is true, then we'd better keep it simple. What kinds of other recyclables are we talking about?''

''Plastic juice and drink bottles,'' proposed Freedom. ''People bring a lot of those to school or buy them in the cafeteria. They're recyclable.''

''Glass is recyclable,'' said Jess, ''but Ms. Hong suggested we not do that for safety reasons. That's why most parents don't pack glass in kids' lunches. And it's a safety risk for us while we handle it, too.''

''We can do paper, though, right?'' asked Vivian. ''From classrooms.''

''That would take a whole new collection system,'' Ramon pointed out. ''And probably more education of people to get past SNEASY.''

''Then paper might be too complicated for now,'' Mr. Montoya suggested.

''Why, Mr. Montoya?'' Cary asked. ''We proved we

71

could recycle cans. We're a pretty good team. I think we're ready for more.''

"I do, too," echoed Freedom. "Cary's right. We can't call ourselves the Eco-kids unless we're really committed."

Ramon shrugged, then got a pinched look on his face. "In that case, why don't we just do *everything*? Recycle for the school, the city, the whole world—"

"Hey, that's it!" Cary interrupted him, sitting bolt upright. "It's been bouncing around in my head all week and I couldn't pin it down. Why don't we recycle in the neighborhood? See, my brother's scout troop picks up the cans and newspapers for their own families, but no one else. Our neighbors throw away their recyclables all the time."

"Hey, I was being sarcastic." Ramon frowned.

"But why not try it?" asked Freedom. "We could recycle in your neighborhood around Opal Street, since that's where our headquarters is."

"Let's be specific here," Mr. Montoya suggested. "It has been proposed that the Eco-kids expand school recycling and begin neighborhood recycling, too."

"That's right," said Vivian. She read back from the notes she had been taking. "Add plastic drink bottles and white paper to school recycling. Start up recycling in the Opal Street neighborhood."

"It seems some of you are strongly in favor, some opposed, and some on the fence about the proposals," observed Mr. Montoya.

"I'm in favor," Freedom said.

Mr. Montoya grinned. "We know that. And Ms. Chen is, too."

Cary nodded enthusiastically.

"I might be," Sienna began, "except that I'm too busy. Don't count on me for much help."

"Don't worry, we know better," Jess assured her. Sienna made a face. "Hah, hah."

Ramon sighed. "Well, I think it's a mistake, but I'll go for it anyway. We're going to drive ourselves nuts."

"Not if we're well organized," Jess put in. "It can work if we arrange it right."

"Ms. Rosenblatt? What do you think?" asked Mr. Montoya.

Vivian bit her lip. "Well, it does seem like a lot of work. But maybe it's better to try too much than too little."

"*Hmm,* well said," replied Mr. Montoya. "Still, I have to agree with Ramon. You might end up regretting so much responsibility. But I won't try to talk you out of it if you're seriously committed."

"Where there's a will, there's a way," said Cary.

Mr. Montoya shrugged. "You people have no lack of ambition, I'll say that. How about we meet again tomorrow to work out the details? As Ms. McCabe suggested, the key to success is going to be a good, well-organized plan."

7

Jess had her doubts about just how good or well-organized a plan the Eco-kids devised when they got together again on Saturday.

Ramon grinned at a copy of the flyer Freedom had just pulled out of his backpack. "Hey, looks great!"

"My mother ran it off on the copy machine at the clinic where she works," Freedom explained. "They use recycled paper." His hair looked tousled and his cheeks pink from the bike ride to Cary's.

The club had decided to meet on the weekend there instead of during school, so that Webb could attend.

"Recycled paper?" Cary repeated. "You mean scratch paper? Has it already been used?" She turned one of the flyers over to see if it had writing on the back.

Freedom shook his head. "No. It's like recycled newspaper. They take regular used paper and mix it up with water and stuff to make new, fresh paper."

"Do you really think the flyers look good?" asked Vivian. "Freedom came up with the words. I just drew it." She had gotten a ride over with Webb and his family's nanny, Marie Claire, on their way from La Jolla.

"Cute illustrations." Sienna pointed at the little drawings of cans next to "aluminum or tin cans," and to the tiny newspaper, complete with minuscule headlines, next to "newspapers" on the list.

The whole thing read:

PLEASE HELP US PROTECT
THE ENVIRONMENT
SATURDAY, OCTOBER 30TH
RECYCLING COLLECTION DAY
ALUMINUM AND TIN CANS,
PLASTIC DRINK BOTTLES,
NEWSPAPERS
PLEASE LEAVE YOUR RECYCLABLES IN BAGS OR
BOXES AT THE CLUB. WE WILL PICK
THEM UP IN THE AFTERNOON. THANK YOU!
THE ECO-KIDS

"October thirtieth," Webb noted. "That's the day before Halloween."

"We should go in costume!" said Ramon.

Vivian shook her head. "Maybe not. People would think we were trick-or-treating."

"What if we wore recycling and ecology costumes," proposed Sienna. "Like, we dress up as soda cans or garbage bags or even trees or something?"

"Hey, yeah!" Ramon got up and started doing his "Everything's Connected" rap dance. "See, we get everyone's attention this way. I can dress up my dog Lefty and Rocky, my cat, in Sherlock Holmes outfits. They

75

could be the—the—garbage sniffers!'' He collapsed in laughter at his own joke.

Jess frowned. ''I think we've got our hands full already.'' Still looking over the flyer, she asked, ''Shouldn't this mention who the Eco-kids are?''

''I was wondering about that, too,'' said Webb. ''Plus I'll bet there are people who don't know how recycling helps the environment. Maybe we should explain that.''

''Maybe,'' agreed Cary. ''But it's too late now. We've got to pass out the flyers today.''

''In the future,'' Jess suggested, ''we should talk more about the flyer before we draw it up.''

Freedom frowned and Vivian's face clouded over.

''I mean, I''—Jess started over—''I think it looks good. Very attractive.''

''Really?'' asked Vivian.

''Definitely,'' Ramon assured her.

''Yes,'' Jess agreed. ''It does. It's just that next time . . . I think there should be more input.''

''Input,'' Freedom repeated, then nodded. ''Okay. You're right. We probably did overlook some important stuff.''

''Speaking of input,'' Sienna broke in. ''After we get all the input from the neighbors—meaning their cans and bottles and newspapers—what do we do with them? How are we going to pick it all up?''

''I got Buck to drive his car,'' answered Cary. ''The rest of us will follow behind on foot and dump the stuff in his trunk.''

''Buck will be there?'' Sienna got a faraway look on her face.

While Sienna was dreaming, Jess shook her head.

76

"Can we really depend on your brother, Cary? He hates giving us rides. You always have to twist his arm."

"What?" Sienna demanded. "You're talking about the person who stood up for us against the Aquarius security guards!"

"She's got a point." Webb grinned. "He not only stood up for us. He sat down for us, too. During the sit-in."

"That doesn't mean he'll show up Saturday," Jess countered. "And even if he does, his car isn't the most reliable vehicle in the world."

Ramon rolled his eyes. "Relax, McCabe, will ya? You worry about everything."

"Another thing . . ." Jess went on, "where are we going to take the recyclables after we collect them? Do we have that planned yet?"

"Sure," Ramon replied. "I talked to Mr. Rinehart and got permission so that we can take each truckload to the bins at school. He said the bin area will be locked 'cause it's a weekend, but he'll let us in on Monday morning to dump it all in."

Jess groaned. "Oh, no. It's going to sit out there till Monday? What if the principal sees it? He warned us about making a mess."

"How would Gormley see it on the weekend?" asked Freedom.

"That's right," said Cary. "He goes fishing. My dad teaches sailing down at the harbor and always sees him out there on his boat."

"Mr. Gormley, fishing?" Sienna grinned. "I can just picture it. In a canvas hat, his potbelly hanging out over the side of the boat . . ."

"Belly button getting sunburned," added Vivian with a giggle.

Jess bit at a fingernail. "We can laugh about Mr. Gormley all we want, but this plan has too many holes in it. We need to have backups."

"Jess, relax, okay?" Sienna patted her hand. "Sometimes you need to just go with the flow. Nothing is ever going to be perfect." She shrugged. "I took this time management seminar with my parents, and the seminar leader said, 'Don't sweat the small stuff.' "

Jess eyed Sienna, jaw firmly set, ready to shoot back a reply. Before she could, though, Cary's little brother, Luke, entered the garage. Flanked by two of his friends, he wore his usual shy smile. His friends, however, looked very different. Matt Parker and Sam Fong scowled.

"You're invading our turf," Matt announced.

"No way," answered Cary. "*We* cleaned out this garage. *We* put in the lamps and the plants and the furniture. It's our headquarters now, and besides, Mom said we could have it."

Sam shook his head. "That's not what we mean. The recycling."

Ramon got it. "Oh, 'cause we're taking over?"

Matt nodded. "*Our* scout troop recycles this neighborhood." He thumped his chest.

"You're only recycling stuff from your own homes," Cary pointed out. "Not anyone else's."

"So? How'd you know we weren't going to branch out?" Sam narrowed his brown eyes at her.

"Well, were you?" Freedom queried.

Matt and Sam looked doubtful. Luke stared at his shoes.

"Listen, listen." Ramon held up his hands like a referee. "This is not a problem, okay? Not a problem. In fact, it's good for everybody. You guys tell your scout leaders that you're working for an environment merit badge 'cause you're going to be part of the Eco-kids neighborhood recycling team."

"They are going to *what?*" Sienna's face contorted.

Ramon looked proud of himself. "See, they help us, we help them. No problem."

"We don't need help," said Jess. "There are plenty of us already."

Matt scrunched up his nose. "Too many girls in this club."

That earned a glare even from good-natured Vivian.

"Too many *what?*" Sienna demanded.

"Nothin'," mumbled the boy, intimidated by the presence of so many older—and bigger—girls.

Jess took that as a hopeful sign. "We really don't need you on this. You would only be in the way."

Immediately she saw her mistake. Some kids liked nothing better than a challenge. To be told they couldn't do something made them want to do it all the more.

"We won't be in the way!" Sam protested.

Sienna hissed, "Jess, haven't you ever heard of reverse psychology?"

Throughout the discussion Luke kept his eyes on his sneakers. Occasionally he stared off into space and whistled softly, as if he'd rather be anywhere else. His friends, however, were very much in the here and now.

"You can't recycle this neighborhood without us!" Matt insisted. "We won't let you. We—we'll mess everything up!"

Ramon stuck two fingers in his mouth and whistled.

"Will everybody just shut up for a minute? Let's have a little cooperation here."

Freedom spoke up. "Well, maybe it wouldn't hurt to let these monkeys hang around."

"Hey! We're no monkeys!" Sam sputtered in outrage.

"Okay, whatever." Freedom waved at them with the back of his hand. "But I agree with Ramon. Let's try a little cooperation here."

More to get the monkeys off their backs than anything else, the rest of the club members finally shrugged in agreement.

"All right, then," Cary agreed. "Sounds like a plan."

Jess sighed. Images of the upcoming neighborhood recycling day played through her mind like a nightmare. Buck Chen as a driver. His rattle trap, breakdown car as their collection vehicle. Obnoxious kid tagalongs. Plus an uncertain collection site at the school. It didn't sound like a plan. It sounded like disaster.

The next day Jess walked up and down Opal Street, Emerald Drive, and Ruby Lane with Webb, leaving a flyer at every house. Some neighbors answered the door to talk about the recycling project—even to congratulate the Eco-kids for starting it. Mr. and Mrs. Sobieski had lots of questions, which Jess and Webb answered while the couple's two preschool children climbed all over them. Penny Allbright, a young woman who had recently moved in a few houses away, told them this was the best news she'd heard in a long time and offered to help any way she could.

At the opposite extreme, Cary's next door neighbor Mr. Wartman scowled when they handed him a flyer, then shut the door in their faces. Other neighbors weren't the least bit interested, and at houses where no one answered, Jess and Webb folded flyers and tucked them into the door frames.

"I wonder how much participation we'll get," said Webb as he left a flyer at the third empty house in a row.

"Anyone's guess," Jess answered. "I'm thinking of this as an experiment."

Webb nodded. "Everything we're doing is an experiment, really. The Eco-kids are trying things no one else has bothered with before. Oh, there's something I forgot to mention yesterday."

Jess lifted an eyebrow.

"Some kids in the science club at my school got pretty interested when I told them about your school's recycling program and the one we're starting here in your neighborhood. Looks like we're going to try one at our school, too."

"Recycling?" Jess smiled. "That's great."

Webb nodded. "And I'm the committee chairperson for it."

"Really, Webb? Congratulations!"

He blushed so hard his freckles faded. "Thanks. I've never been the head of anything before."

"Oh, you'll do fine," Jess assured him.

As they walked along, Jess glanced at Webb. He didn't look much different than he had last year in sixth grade—same red hair, freckles, blue eyes. Sometimes he was so quiet that he just blended in with the background—you hardly noticed him. Still, Jess knew that on the inside Webb had changed over the summer. In the beginning it had seemed hard for him to speak up in conversations or at Five Cat Club meetings. But now he planned to run a whole recycling program!

Maybe that was what belonging to a club did for him, Jess thought. It changed him. Taught him things. How, Jess wondered, was the Eco-kids changing her?

Before school Monday morning she wished very much that something would change her sister. Or even that something would come and take Beth away. The giant squid from *Twenty Thousand Leagues Under the Sea*, or maybe something less drastic, like the tornado in *The Wizard of Oz*.

That sounded good. Beth could be carried off to Oz, leaving Jess to enjoy a peaceful breakfast with her family.

She'd never had mean thoughts about Beth before (or at least not quite such mean thoughts) until the day at the mall with Kandi. Since that day over a week before, she and Beth hadn't spoken. They'd pass in the hall or on the stairs, seemingly not noticing each other's existence.

At breakfast on Monday, their mother announced that she'd had enough.

"You girls are getting on my nerves." Mama folded the morning paper with a slap. "What is this feud about? Whatever it is, it's ridiculous."

Jess frowned, silently blaming Mama's outburst on Beth, who had asked Dad to pass the salt shaker even though Jess was sitting right by it. Up until then, it seemed Mama and Dad hadn't noticed.

Unfortunately, they had.

"I'm tired of it, too," Dad muttered between swallows of orange juice. He popped a vitamin tablet in his mouth and swallowed again. "Whatever the problem is between you two, it can't be that serious."

Grammy nodded. "Amen to that."

How nice to have so many experts in the family, thought Jess.

Claiming that she would be late for her ride to school, Beth jumped up and hurried out the front door with her books.

Of course, three heads turned to Jess, expecting answers.

"Oops! Sienna and Cary will be waiting for me." Jess started to push back her chair but felt her mother's firm grip on her arm.

"Sienna is *never* waiting," Mama pointed out. "You have plenty of time."

"Yes, but . . ." Jess stammered. Wasn't it just like Beth to scoot out and leave her holding the bag!

A look passed from Grammy to Mama, who finally let Jess go.

"There will be time for talking later," Grammy said softly, as if speaking to Curie, who played with a ribbon in her lap.

Jess nodded and kissed everyone good-bye.

Maybe there would be a talk later. Mama, Grammy, Dad . . . somebody would corner her eventually. But one thing was certain in Jess's mind. She would never, ever speak to her sister again.

"This is going to be a big mess." Mr. Gormley sighed heavily, as if the tons of recyclable materials pressed down on his chest. The principal slumped in his big leather chair, tired gray eyes avoiding contact with the Eco-kids assembled in his office.

"Not really, Mr. Gormley," said Freedom. "To collect the white paper all we need is one box in each classroom and office. For the plastic bottles all we need are a few new boxes next to the ones we've already got out for the aluminum cans."

During the past ten minutes Freedom, Jess, and Vivian, who had volunteered to speak with Mr. Gormley about expanding the school recycling program, had been giving him excellent reasons for the idea. It would help the environment, it would help students learn responsibility, it could save the school money, and even make a little money for the school. For every reason in favor of the idea, Mr. Gormley came up with two of his own—against.

"Overburdening the teachers," he intoned. "They've got enough to worry about without having to keep track of old paper, too."

"They won't have to worry about it at all," said Jess. "Our club will. We'll go into the classrooms on certain days every week to pick up the contributions."

Leaning against a bookcase, Mr. Montoya cleared his throat. "Speaking as a teacher myself, Mr. Gormley, and having run the idea past the other teachers, there really doesn't seem to be a problem with this. Students in my classes will either deposit their used white paper in the boxes or they won't. It's not the teacher's job to monitor that. The Eco-kids are assuming full responsibility for collection."

"But will they live up to it?" Mr. Gormley gazed at the teacher above the heads of the club members, as if they weren't even there. "Or is this school going to turn into some sort of garbage experiment, smothering

84

under mountains of rubbish that no one gets around to picking up?''

The Eco-kids glanced at each other. Freedom scowled, and Vivian was having a hard time holding back a giggle. Jess felt like laughing, too. Mr. Gormley often came up with hilarious statements, owing to the fact that he liked to exaggerate.

Finally Jess cleared her throat. ''Our aluminum can recycling program has been in place for a month now, Mr. Gormley. Has that made a mess?''

The principal drummed his fingers on the desk. His salt-and-pepper crew cut bristled up like porcupine quills.

''The program has run very smoothly,'' Jess continued, answering her own questions. ''Successfully, too. We've gotten an excellent response from students. If we can handle the cans, there's no reason why we can't handle other materials, too.''

For the first time so far, Mr. Gormley focused his eyes on the kids. ''This aluminum can thing—I allowed that on a trial basis.'' He sighed. ''And that's how this will be as well. All right? We'll try it for one month. But if it causes any trouble at all . . .''

''It won't,'' Vivian promised, grinning. ''Don't worry. It'll go great.''

Mr. Gormley nodded tiredly, like a man who had heard it all before.

''Thank you, Mr. Gormley,'' they chorused politely as they left his office.

Walking down the hall outside, the Eco-kids and Mr. Montoya raised their hands and gave each other high-five slaps.

*   *   *

85

On her way to the headquarters Saturday morning, Jess expected a lot of excitement. After all, it was the first neighborhood recycling day. But she didn't expect the flurry that greeted her when she entered the Chens' garage.

Ramon handed her a piece of gray stationery that had come in the mail to Cary's house.

"It's got all our names on it," Jess noted.

"Almost all," Webb pointed out. "They don't know about the new members yet."

Vivian sagged a little.

"Oh, but I'm sure you can go, too," Ramon assured her. "The Southern California Marine Mammal Association is a great group."

Jess read aloud. " 'You and your families are cordially invited to attend a party to celebrate the successful liberation of the (former) Aquarius dolphins. November seventh, five P.M.' "

"Awesome, huh?" Ramon made a thumbs-up sign.

Jess read the rest of the note to herself. *The Five Cat Club members were the keys to our success. We hope you can all come! Sincerely, Harvey Edelman, director of education, Southern California Marine Mammal Association.*

"Tell me again," said Freedom, unstrapping his bicycle helmet. "How'd you get Aquarius Marine Park to turn the dolphins over to the SCMMA?"

Webb shook his head. "It wasn't easy. We had to—"

"Can we go into this some other time?" Cary interrupted. She had been fidgeting, and now seemed to lose all patience. "We've got stuff to do."

"Like what?" Ramon looked at his watch. "Recycling pickup time isn't till noon. It's only eleven now."

"Are we going to wait till then to get ready?" demanded Cary.

"Buck's not even here yet," Jess pointed out. "Where is he, by the way?"

"He'll be here," said Cary, avoiding the question. "We're supposed to line his car trunk with plastic so the recyclables won't mess it up."

Jess breathed deeply. At least the car was there. Buck couldn't be too far away.

"I thought the monkeys were supposed to get the trunk ready," said Ramon.

Freedom shrugged. "Looks like they're not here yet, either."

"Maybe it'll stay that way," Jess muttered, "if we're lucky."

"How about Sienna?" asked Webb. "Where is she?"

"She said she'd be here at noon," Vivian reported.

"Sleeping late," noted Jess.

Cary shrugged. "Come on. Let's fix the trunk."

Six people trying to line a car trunk with garbage bags did not work. They got in one another's way and bickered. Finally Cary took over to do it herself while the others watched.

After a few minutes the monkeys burst out of the kitchen, true to the name. Following them came the Chens' dogs, barking and darting about to greet everyone. Sienna showed up around the same time that Buck emerged from the house to "warm up" his car. That consisted of his trying to start it several times, then getting out and fiddling with something under the hood, then getting back in and trying to start it again. After several coughs, sputters, and groans, it finally came alive.

87

In spite of the fact that Buck hadn't combed his hair and seemed to have slept in his clothes, Sienna couldn't take her eyes off him long enough to listen to his sister, Cary, who was ordering everyone around like an army general.

Jess sighed. All in all, it seemed to her that the Eco-kids' first neighborhood recycling day was getting off to a shaky start. Not that it was all the younger boys' fault or the dogs' or Buck's or Sienna's or Cary's. The old saying, "Too many cooks spoil the broth" kept coming to mind.

A mob of ten people trotted along behind Buck's car down Opal Street, gathering the generous amounts of recyclables that neighbors had set out. At least no one could complain about participation. Three out of four houses had left bags or boxes for them. Still, arguments broke out over where in the trunk to put the different materials, what to do about the "mistakes," or items that couldn't be recycled, and whose fault it was when a bag full of cans and newspapers broke open and spilled all over the sidewalk.

To top it off, Gina and Patti ambushed them at the end of the block. Of course, they wanted to "help." And of course, no one wanted them to—least of all Matt and Sam, who made that very clear by shoving at the girls. Matt knocked Patti off her bike. Patti cried, loudly, for a long time, despite Vivian's best efforts to comfort her. The little girl only shut up when Cary gave in and told her that she and her friend could help.

And all that was just on Opal Street. Webb and Cary went with Buck to take the first trunk load of recyclables to the school. The others waited at the headquarters, trying to prevent the boys from pelting the girls with dirt clods and the girls from kicking the boys' shins.

"Never had so much fun," Freedom grumbled.

"Why, oh why, are these children here?" groaned Sienna.

"*You* try and get rid of them," said Jess.

Sienna didn't try anything, because Buck's old clunker roared up in front of the house. He leaned on his horn—the custom kind that went *ah-ooh-gah!*—as if no one had noticed he was there.

"Come on!" he yelled. "I can't spend all day on this."

The recycling brigade trotted down Opal to Emerald Drive and began the whole process again there.

The day might have gone okay after all, if it hadn't been for the strange sounds that started coming from Buck's car engine about halfway up Emerald.

"What's that?" Jess asked him.

Buck shrugged. "What's what?"

"Yeah, I hear it," said Ramon, "in your engine, Buck. Sounds like somebody's coughing in there. *Uh-krr, uh-krr.* Like that."

Buck shrugged again. "I dunno. Just get busy and haul the stuff into the trunk, okay? Can't spend all day out here."

On the way back from dumping the Emerald Drive trunk load at the junior high, the *uh-krr uh-krr* sound got worse. The car shivered, shook, and died at the corner of Opal and Crown Avenue.

"It was like a last gasp," reported Webb after he and Cary walked back to the headquarters. "The car's last words."

"Where's Buck?" asked Sienna.

89

"Out there mourning," Cary answered. "And waiting for his friends to help him push it home."

"What do we do now?" Vivian wondered. "We can't leave all that stuff at people's curbs."

Phone calls to parents turned up no one able to help. This was just too short notice to round up volunteers. Cary's parents were both working all day, as were Sienna's. Webb's *au pair* had the day off. Neither his parents nor Ramon's mother nor Vivian's father wanted to haul garbage in their cars. Jess's father offered his van, but only after the TV football game ended in the evening.

"We shouldn't wait that long." Freedom shook his head. "It'll make a bad impression. The neighbors won't want their garbage sitting around all day."

"What choice do we—" began Webb, but was interrupted by what sounded like the approach of a small army.

Before then, Jess hadn't noticed that the little girls were missing.

Gina, Patti, and two of their friends marched up the driveway, rolling an assortment of doll carriages, mini-dump trucks, and little red wagons behind them.

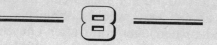

"I've never seen so much paper in my life." On Sunday afternoon, Sienna stared boggle-eyed at a mountain of *Jewel Beach Journal* newspapers. The stacks stood a little taller than she did and took up a picnic blanket-sized space in the vacant lot next door to Cary's house.

Alongside the newspapers, lumpy paper bags full of cans made a smaller mountain, and next to that sat a little hill of recyclable plastics.

"We got the best response for newspaper," Jess observed. "Maybe because people are used to the idea of that being recycled."

"We'll just have to help them get used to the idea of the other stuff, too," said Cary with a firm nod.

Jess wondered how, exactly, the Eco-kids recycling crew could handle even more cans and plastics. Collecting just this had taken all Saturday afternoon. Following up on Gina and Patti's idea, the older kids had borrowed their families' wheelbarrows and garden carts. The Eco-kids, large and small, had spent four hours trundling load after load of recyclables back to headquarters. It sounded like a roller derby and looked like a ragtag parade, making such a spectacle that some of the neighbors came out to watch.

91

When it became clear that the Chens' garage couldn't contain the whole collection, someone pointed out the vacant lot.

Now, the following day, Jess realized there was still too much left to do for this week's collection before worrying about next week's. She had changed her clothes and rushed over right after church and Sunday dinner. In just a few minutes her father and Cary's mother would drive over to help transfer the piles of recyclables from the vacant lot to the school.

Like a sculptor examining her latest piece, Sienna stepped back to admire the three mounds. "Funny, to feel so proud of a bunch of garbage."

They all laughed. And Jess agreed—she was proud. Saturday's collection effort had left her feeling tired, sore, and very accomplished.

"Not really garbage," Cary corrected her, "recyclable garbage."

"Yeah, our gold mine," said Sienna. "Isn't it funny, too, how the three of us always find such valuable things in trash heaps?"

"Hey, that's right." Cary grinned. "We found the kittens here—in a trash heap there at the back of the lot."

Jess nodded. "This is where it all started. The kittens, then the Five Cat Club . . ."

"And now the Eco-kids!" added Cary.

"Hi, Sienna!" called someone from the sidewalk. "Happy Halloween!"

"Mandy! Hi!" Sienna waved to the pretty blond girl. "Happy Halloween!"

Mandy shaded her eyes from the sun. "Want to go to Kendra's with me? She said you could come. We're going to the beach to rehearse our Princess and the Pea lines, and later we're going to Heather Connell's Halloween party.''

Sienna started for the sidewalk. "You mean the *eighth grade* party?"

Cary caught her elbow. "We have to load this stuff into my mom's and Jess's dad's cars to take to the school."

"Can't you get Ramon to help?" Sienna asked.

"He *is* going to help us," said Jess. "We need all the help we can get."

"Listen, you guys, I never said I'd work on this today. I told you from the beginning that you should count me mostly out on this project, remember? I've already done plenty. I helped all day yesterday—"

"Because your dreamboat Bucky was there," Jess muttered.

"Well, I was helping, wasn't I?" Sienna pursed her lips. "Come on, you guys. Don't be so possessive."

"Possessive?" Cary wrinkled her nose.

"I've got other friends and other things to do, you know? I mean, I still want to spend time with you guys, but I don't want to be an Eco-kid one hundred percent of my time."

"Sienna, you coming?" Mandy called.

Jess couldn't think of a way to argue with Sienna. Maybe she was right. No one ever said members had to donate all their free time to the club.

"See you later, okay?" Sienna looked them both squarely in the eyes, as if asking an important question.

Jess realized that it *was* an important question. Although she resented Sienna goofing off when there was work to do, and even resented her a little for goofing

93

off with other friends, she forced herself to nod. "Okay, see you later."

Cary nodded, too. Then Sienna gave them a relieved smile and hurried away with Mandy.

"Gina and the other monkeys put in more work than she did yesterday," Cary grumbled.

Jess shrugged. It was true. Sienna was no powerhouse of manual labor. Still, she had warned them she wouldn't be. They couldn't hold that against her now. She started to say so, but a booming bellow stopped her.

"What do you children think you're doing over there?"

They turned to find Mr. Wartman on the upper balcony of his house next door to Cary's, pointing down at them.

"Is this some kind of Halloween prank?"

Meanwhile, Ramon was crossing the street toward the vacant lot, hands in pockets. "We're recycling," he hollered back.

"I don't care what you call it," yelled Mr. Wartman. "I call it making a mess. I don't want it next door to my house."

"It's not next door to your house, Mr. Wartman," Jess pointed out. "It's next door to the Chens'."

"Don't sass me!" he roared.

Ramon rolled his eyes. "Is he always this way?"

Cary shrugged. "*Mrs.* Wartman was really nice, but she died last year, and now Mr. Wartman has nothing better to do than grouch at people. It's no use us trying to talk with him. Oh, good, there's my mom. She can handle him."

Ms Chen pulled her old blue car up to the curb with Jess's father close behind in the McCabes' new van.

"Hi, everybody." Cary's mom smiled as she got out. She had come dressed for the job in jeans, a work shirt, and rubber gloves.

Jess's father, who didn't even own a pair of jeans, looked almost ready for a day at his insurance office in the pressed slacks and dress shoes he'd worn to church.

"Hello there, Mr. Wartman," Dad called with a wave up at their neighbor.

"Listen down there," the older man commanded. "We can't have this kind of thing on our street, you hear me? We have a good street. A quiet neighborhood. Those children are turning it into bedlam. Making all that racket yesterday afternoon. Then I wake up this morning to find that junk piled up next door. As if there weren't enough trash there already! It's a vacant lot, not the city dump!"

"Sorry, Mr. Wartman," said Cary's mom. "We'll haul it away now."

Ignoring her, Mr. Wartman went on. "It's been there all night and half the day. What are those children doing—trying to ruin this neighborhood? Drive property values down?"

"You're right, Mr. Wartman. We apologize. It will all be gone in a bit." Ms. Chen smiled.

"He's *right?*" Jess repeated, frowning.

Cary tugged on her mother's sleeve. "Mom, aren't you going to explain to him about our recycling project?"

"He's not *right*—he's a grump," Ramon muttered.

"Now, come on, everybody." Jess's father directed them toward the piles of recyclables. "Let's get this show on the road, all right? Let's not cause any more annoyance to our neighbors."

Jess followed him, shaking her head. Some people just didn't understand the importance of recycling—like Mr. Wartman. How could the Eco-kids get through to him? And what if the recycling project had to use the vacant lot again next Saturday? That seemed very likely, considering the fact that Buck's car showed no signs of recovery, and that no one else was available to drive on Saturdays. Sunday morning would be the earliest they could haul their collection to the school. Meanwhile, it had to sit somewhere, and the vacant lot was the only choice.

Planning, thought Jess. If only the club had done more of it before launching this project.

Carrying two arm loads of plastic milk jugs to her father's van, she sighed. No sense in dwelling on it now. Hundreds of cans, bottles, and newspapers waited for a ride to school.

"Do I look okay?" Sienna fussed with her green spangled bow tie. She wore her hair piled on top of her head, jade eyeshadow, and frosty pink lipstick.

"You look like a movie star," said Cary, "on her way to the Academy Awards."

"That is kind of how it feels tonight," agreed Vivian, wearing a flowery jumper. "Doesn't it? Like we're going to the Academy Awards!"

Jess nodded, grinning. "It is exciting."

Although Sienna was the most glamorous among them, all the Eco-kids members had dressed up at least a little for the SCMMA party. Jess had worn her black pants, a red plaid blouse, and a little of Mama's red lipstick. Everyone clustered in front of the old Victorian house that served as the SCMMA headquarters near downtown San Diego, a half-hour drive from Jewel Beach. Jess's father couldn't come because of a meeting, but Cary, Ramon, and their mothers had car-pooled with Jess and hers.

"This is going to be funny," said Ramon, "when we walk in like a mob."

"But a famous mob," Sienna added.

With that, Ramon led the march up the front steps. He hadn't had time to ring the bell yet when the door opened.

Jess swallowed nervously. She had attended awards ceremonies for students at school, but never a big, official, grown-up party.

"Hello!" A heavy-set woman in yellow stood in the doorway. "Welcome!" She peered around Ramon to the rest of the group and smiled. "You must be the Five Cat Club!"

Sienna stepped forward. "The *former* Five Cat Club. Hi. I'm Sienna Sabo. We're called the Eco-kids now."

"Eco-kids. That's wonderful. I'm Pat Jackson, executive director of SCMMA. It's a pleasure to have you all with us tonight. Please, come in."

The Eco-kids and their parents crowded into the small entryway, where Ms. Jackson helped them off with their coats and ushered them into an even more crowded adjoining room. There, a long banner reading VICTORY! ran across the wall, with a buffet table spread out under it.

Jess quickly forgot her jitters. There was so much going on—staff members introducing themselves, offering them food, wanting to know more about the Eco-kids—that she found herself feeling very adult and confident. She could have been just another environmentalist. No one here seemed to notice that the Eco-kids were, after all, just kids. She couldn't imagine the education director, Harvey Edelman, who personally greeted each Eco-kid, yelling at them the way Mr. Wartman had. She couldn't imagine anyone here ignoring her the way Beth had done. Here, a kid got some respect.

"Look, it's Leon!" Webb pointed at one of the large photos on the wall. A gleaming, blue-black dolphin leapt high over a turquoise sea.

"Is that the dolphin you saved?" asked Sienna's father.

"One of them." Sienna held her chin up proudly.

"And there's Tamara." Cary pointed at the next photo.

They all gathered around the series of a half-dozen pictures of the dolphins swimming, jumping, and nuzzling one another.

"What gorgeous animals," commented Ms. Chen.

"We thought the Eco-kids would enjoy seeing some of the results of their work," explained Harvey, gesturing toward the photos. "As you can see, Tamara's doing great. In this picture she's interacting easily with the other dolphins. Leon's progressing more slowly. The protected habitat may turn out to be his permanent home. Tamara's chances for eventual release back into the wild look better, because she's re-adapting much more easily so far. But the habitat is ideal for them both right now, very much like the real ocean but without the dangers. It's a large acreage of shore waters, perfect for rehabilitating once-captive dolphins, separated from the open ocean only by the wire fence you see here."

"Oh, and the staff at the habitat made up a scrapbook," added Ms. Jackson. She opened an album to a photo of Leon in a big sling, being lowered by crane into the water.

The caption for the next photo—of Leon swimming out of the sling, read, *Leon tastes the sea again!*

"Later we'll show you a video the habitat staff made." Ms. Jackson grinned. "They call it 'Leon and Tamara's Greatest Hits,' which includes Tam catching her first live fish in years!"

Jess's mother slipped an arm around her daughter and whispered, "I had no idea the extent of what your club has accomplished. I wish your father could have been here tonight."

After they'd all had plates of pizza and sandwiches, Harvey asked, "How about a tour of our offices? They're not pretty but they're functional."

He was right. The walls needed a new coat of paint. Some of the window blinds hung at a lopsided half mast, as if they hadn't opened properly in years. Here or there someone had tacked up a colorful poster or tucked in a potted plant in an attempt to make things more homey, but there wasn't space for much more. Every room in the house was crammed full of desks, filing cabinets, bookshelves, and big tables covered with paperwork.

"I wonder if *our* headquarters is going to end up looking like this someday," Cary whispered as they climbed the stairs to the second floor.

The very idea of that made Jess shudder.

Harvey read their minds. "I know it looks like a train wreck," he admitted. "But there is some method to our madness here." He went on to explain the work done in each room. There were the research, education, and media relations departments downstairs, and the political action and administration areas on the second floor. "We rarely make a move on anything without a big

99

powwow. We brainstorm, then decide who does what. We've found this system works very well to ensure that we never go off half-cocked on a project, finding ourselves unprepared. And we don't waste valuable time and energy getting in each other's way.''

Jess listened closely to that part. Then Harvey added something even more interesting.

''One of the problems a group like ours can encounter, if we're not careful, is getting stretched too thin. Sometimes we can take on too much and then aren't able to keep up with all the goals we set for ourselves. That can lead to great frustration, even burn out, where our staff and volunteers get tired of trying.''

A couple of staff members grinned and nodded in confirmation.

''So what we aim for,'' Harvey went on, ''is a small number of important projects we know we can complete to some successful degree. And we set up each project very carefully to be run by the right number of people with the right skills and talents.''

He led them to a closet-sized copy room, then opened a door to a flowery terrace with a view down the hillside to downtown and the harbor beyond.

''When things get hectic, this is the therapy area. A few minutes out here and you're almost as good as new.''

Jess watched the nighttime twinkling of lights in the harbor as the sea rocked the distant boats. A plane came in to land at the airport a few miles away. In another direction, the Coronado Bridge made a broad arch over the Pacific. When a stiff, salty breeze whipped up from the water, almost everyone herded back inside. Jess lingered. The breeze and some of Harvey's words seemed to clear her head. She realized she had begun to understand some things that had been a muddle before. The problems with neighborhood recycling day, the floundering recycling program at school . . .

Vivian poked her head back out from the copy room. "C'mon, Jess. Everybody's downstairs. They're going to show the video and make some speeches thanking us and everything."

Following Vivian inside, Jess knew that at the next Eco-kids meeting she would have to make a speech of her own.

One thing Jess felt no clearer on was her sister's idiotic behavior.

After the SCMMA party, she could hardly wait to tell Grammy all about it. . . . Harvey's speech calling the Eco-kids "young champions of the environment," the video of Leon and Tamara, on which the habitat staffers personally thanked the Five Cat Club for their help freeing the dolphins. And at the end each Eco-kid had been presented with framed photos of Leon and Tamara swimming around in their new home, plus little metal pendants in the shape of dolphins. She had walked into her family's house as if on air. But it didn't take long for Beth to bring her back down to earth.

"Let me see your pendant, Jess," she said. "Cute. Is it silver?"

If Jess hadn't been in such a light mood from the party she would have had the good sense not to respond. But she handed the dolphin to her sister.

"Oh. I figured. Just silver plated." Beth handed back the pendant as if it were a gum machine trinket not worthy of her interest.

Like a popped balloon, Jess felt herself sink. A fabulous evening and all it took was one word from her horrible sister to ruin it!

"Jess, come here for a minute." Grammy took her hand and wheeled down to her room.

Curie followed Jess and jumped into her lap on Grammy's bed. Jess was glad to have something to hold on to.

"Now, don't you mind what your sister says, you hear?" Grammy began.

"I don't want to talk about it," Jess answered, pursing her lips. But she didn't get up. She knew better. Grammy would just collar her again.

"Elizabeth is going through a stage. It's an ugly stage, I'll admit, but it'll pass." Grammy patted Jess's knee. "Now. Your mother has spoken to her—"

"She's spoken to Beth?" Jess groaned. "About me?"

"Yes, about you. You don't think a mother is going to let her daughter get away with behaving the way Beth has, do you?"

Jess shrugged.

"Well, she's not. But it's going to take Beth a while to come around, and you just need to be patient, all right? Don't let her get your goat."

It was a little late for that. Beth already had her goat—tied and strung up, too.

But she just nodded. "Yes, Grammy." She wouldn't have admitted it, but it did feel good to know that someone cared about her unhappiness with her sister. Several times she had wanted to talk it out with someone, but who? Cary had been too gung-ho on Eco-kids projects lately. Sienna lived in the ozone with her drama group and her new friends. Even Mama seemed too busy.

Jess looked at her grandmother, at her dark face, her

brown eyes, and realized there was at least one person willing to listen.

She took a deep breath. "I wish . . . I wish I could make Beth like me again."

Grammy shook her head, eyes soft. She reached a hand out to Jess and wheeled closer. "I can't hold you on my lap, sugar, but I'm going to hold your hand."

Jess nodded, eyes glued on Curie so that Grammy wouldn't see the tears pooling. "Doesn't Beth know how mean she is?"

"Now you hold on to me, girl. Hold fast."

Jess took a big sniff.

Grammy's strong fingers wrapped tight around her own. "Maybe your sister doesn't know how much she's hurt you. Sometimes people are too caught up in themselves to see outside. And sometimes we ourselves can be too good at hiding things." She leaned closer and lifted Jess's chin. "Sometimes we just don't want to show them how much they've hurt us. But listen. All you ever, ever need to worry about in this life is one thing. Just one thing. Not about Beth liking you. Not about what anyone else in the whole world thinks of you. All you have to answer to is one thing. And that one thing"— Grammy touched a finger to Jess's heart.—"that one thing is what you see when you look right in here."

Curie mewed and stretched both paws up to bat at Grammy's finger. A giggle broke through Jess's sad cloud.

"Well, you're nothing but a bother, aren't you?" Grammy asked the kitten fondly. Then she drew Jess into a hug. "Come here, sugar."

Snug in her grandmother's arms, holding Curie in her own, Jess could no longer fight the tears. They came slowly, like a soft, welcome rain.

9

Glancing in the mirror Monday morning, Jess decided she looked like a goldfish. Puffy eyes, swollen cheeks, a sad mouth—that's what crying on Grammy's shoulder last night had done to her.

On the inside, though, she felt much better. Grammy's comfort had helped a lot. Maybe she should have let the tears flow long before, even in front of Beth. Maybe everyone, not just Grammy, needed to see that Jess McCabe had feelings, too.

Something Ramon had said weeks ago echoed in her ears. "You're always thinking, McCabe. What an amazing brain you are."

Was that how people saw her—as just a brain, no heart?

Jess combed and rebraided her hair, considering the question. A person who read a lot, won math and science awards, and played chess would probably be thought of as "brainy." If that individual also liked to be practical and well organized, and tended to speak out when things didn't work out that way, others might form impressions of the person based on those facts alone, ignoring other parts of the individual's personality.

She pinned the braids over her head, nodding at her

reflection. It all made sense. For instance, those days when Cary didn't notice that she wanted to talk. And why her own sister thought she could handle being snubbed. Not even Mama had picked up on just how hurt she had been feeling. Just as Grammy said, Jess was pretty good at hiding it. Life felt easier when you just ignored things that troubled you, hoping they'd go away.

Well, so far no giant squid or *Wizard of Oz* tornado had taken Beth away. Chances were they never would. Sisters forever, Jess and Beth were stuck with each other.

A beep from her programmed wristwatch reminded Jess that she was two minutes behind her dressing schedule. Pulling a blue sweater over her blouse, she thought back to her grandmother's advice. If it was true that all a person had to answer to was what she found in her own heart, did that mean she didn't need to get along with others? Didn't need to change to please them, or to try and show them who she really was?

She zipped up her tote bag and started for the kitchen. Reaching the stairwell, she heard a car horn honk, and watched Beth rush out the front door.

Oh, well. For the moment, some of her questions would have to go unanswered.

Freedom shook his head at the recycling box in Mr. Montoya's classroom. "Look at that. It's almost empty."

Recovering from a cold, Vivian sneezed, then said, "Or just a little full, depending on how you look at it."

"I'd like to take that attitude," Jess said, "but I agree with Freedom. We're not getting much of a response to our white paper recycling effort."

It was the regular Wednesday meeting, but the mood was more like what you'd find at a funeral.

"Freedom and I checked through all the classrooms yesterday," said Ramon. "A couple of them even had *nothing* in the box."

"Actually, one of them had an athletic sock in it"— Freedom made a face—"recently worn."

"Hmm." Mr. Montoya stroked his beard. "And the aluminum can count has fallen off, too?"

"Way off, this week," Jess reported. "Even less than last week."

"A steady decline after the tremendous response earlier," Mr. Montoya noted. "Well, there's something else to discuss, too. Ms. Chen has discovered a problem that needs input."

Jess realized that Cary hadn't said a word yet during the meeting. Looking at her now, she saw a face as long as a mile.

Fiddling with a pencil eraser, Cary began, "There is a problem. A big one." Her mouth was set in a firm little line, and her cheeks began to color. "I got yelled at yesterday by Mr. Gormley."

"For what?" asked Jess.

"For something that wasn't my fault." Cary looked up, pinning each member with her gaze. "I got in trouble because of the mess we left outside the bin area Sunday."

"You mean the neighborhood recyclables we left there?" Ramon asked. "Gormley already knew we were going to do that. We cleared it with him and with the custodian. What's the big deal?"

"The big deal," Cary replied, "is that the recyclables had to stay there until Monday afternoon, because *you*

106

weren't around to help move it into the bins. Guess who walked by and saw it? Guess who went on and on to me about how he knew all along our club was going to end up making a mess? Mr. Gormley! You know, Ramon, you and Freedom and Vivian were supposed to be there Monday morning to transfer the stuff into the bins. None of you showed up. Jess and I ended up doing it, but we didn't have a free period to do it in till after lunch."

"Cary, I was at home sick that day," Vivian defended herself in the middle of a cough.

Ramon held his hands out. "I had to cram for a math test. I thought Vivian and Freedom could handle it."

Freedom shrugged. "And I forgot all about it. What can I say? I already apologized."

Cary's eyes darted from one to the other. "I'm tired of excuses. The fact is that because you all flubbed up—"

"I did not flub up!" Vivian protested. "I was sick!"

"Because nobody showed up," Cary went on, "I got stuck with the extra work, and I got yelled at."

"Don't you mean *we?*" Jess corrected. "*We* got stuck with the extra work? Mr. Rinehart and I helped, too, remember?"

"Well, but you didn't get yelled at."

Mr. Montoya made a wry face. "If it's any consolation to you, Ms. Chen, I got yelled at, too."

"Wow. Gormley yelled at *you?*" Ramon's eyes widened.

"Let's just say Mr. Gormley spoke to me about the situation of the recyclables being left outside the bin area. And he was not pleased."

Cary was still frowning, arms crossed. "I'm tired of

107

doing other people's jobs, of keeping things going. This club needs to shape up.''

Never one to mince words, Ramon said, ''You're nuts. We do lots of work. I, personally, spent most of my weekend on club stuff. On Saturday, who kept the little kids from killing each other, huh? And on Sunday, who spent lots of time helping you and Jess haul the stuff to school? Huh? Huh? Just who was that?''

Cary went on glaring at him.

''Ramon has a point,'' Freedom put in. ''We all work hard on the club stuff. I really am sorry I forgot about Monday morning—''

''Fat lot of good being sorry does,'' Cary muttered. ''Everything's falling apart—school recycling, neighborhood recycling . . .''

Ramon shook his head. ''Ease up, Chen. Things aren't that bad. But you hassle us constantly. If it's not one thing, it's another.''

''Yeah,'' echoed Freedom. ''Like that thing with Matt on Saturday. The kid was using his paper route bike for the collection, and you complained he wasn't picking up enough stuff. So he filled his sacks to the brim and when they spilled over in the street you nailed him for that, too.''

''It's true, Cary. Nothing's been good enough for you.'' Vivian blew her nose.

Cary listened in stony silence. Jess kept trying to think of something to say in defense of her friend. The truth was that before the Eco-kids started, Cary had been a pretty easygoing person. These days she was a pain in the neck.

At the moment, Cary looked a lot like Mr. Gormley— tired, frustrated, carrying the weight of the world on her shoulders. The word "burn-out" came to Jess's mind. Harvey Edelman had warned them that it sometimes happened when people worked too hard for too few results. Jess realized that description fit Cary just right. Glancing around at the tense, wary faces of the other club members, she decided they looked a bit singed, too.

This seemed like a perfect time to make the speech she'd thought of at the SCMMA party. But just then Sienna breezed in.

"Why, thanks for joining us, Sienna," snapped Cary. "Only twenty minutes late."

"Aren't we in a lovely mood?" Sienna chirped.

"We were just talking about that," said Ramon. "How easy Cary is to get along with these days."

Jess stepped in. "Tone it down. Let's not pick on Cary."

Ramon turned to look at her. "Okay. You're no prize-winner lately, either, McCabe."

Jess opened her mouth to reply, but Freedom jumped in. "Right, like the way you want to keep the recyclable piles in the vacant lot so neat. Just so. What difference does it make?"

Sienna leaned her head to the side. "You know, I went to a seminar on just this topic, Shedding Your Skin—How to Let Go and Step Out. About people's lives getting hung up on certain personality traits, like—"

That was when Jess nearly hit the ceiling. She couldn't stand it when Sienna came up with her pop psychology and New Age and psychic healing and who-knew-what theories. Somehow, though, she managed to hold her tongue and think before speaking. Somebody had to stop this discussion before it turned into any more of a verbal brawl.

109

She cleared her throat. "Ahem. Excuse me. I need to say something."

Several faces turned toward her and none of them looked happy. She almost chickened out. This wasn't exactly a receptive audience.

"Well, um, its sounds like we're all upset," she began, "and for some good reasons, too. I think we're all getting on each others' nerves."

"Hmph," Ramon snorted. "You can say that again."

Jess ignored him. "I keep thinking back to things Harvey Edelman said about the SCMMA. Some of it sounds similar to problems we've had. Like us, the SCMMA is often tempted to take on too many projects. It's hard to back away from important things—like saving dolphins or preventing ocean pollution or whatever. So they have to narrow it down to what they know they can handle, and then they have to make sure and stay really organized on it, plan it out carefully."

A few faces were scowling, but at least everyone was still listening to her.

"Now, I know I've got a reputation for being super-organized and punctual and all, and it appears that can be irritating to people. I guess, well, I shouldn't expect everyone to do things the way I would do them."

"Exactly." Sienna nodded. "I couldn't have said it better."

Jess went on. "What I'm getting at is I think we've each got special skills."

That earned an encouraging nod from Mr. Montoya.

"For instance, maybe my talent is for organizing things. And Vivian is really good at making posters and things for us. Everybody has something they do well."

"Hmm." Freedom looked at her thoughtfully. "I re-

110

member Harvey Edelman talking about this—how the SCMMA divides their work up into different departments according to people's skills.''

Jess took heart. ''Right. That's what I mean. Maybe we're not putting our individual talents to good enough use. We bounce from project to project without setting up the right teams for them first. I think that's why we're hitting so many snags in both school and neighborhood recycling.''

''But we planned those out plenty,'' Ramon objected. ''Lots of meetings, lots of talk.''

''That's true.'' Jess nodded. ''But maybe we didn't think ahead enough to things that could go wrong.''

Freedom shrugged. ''I see your point. For school recycling, we assumed we could just add paper and plastic onto the success of the aluminum cans, without spreading the word about them first. It didn't work. People haven't caught on.''

''*I* wasn't the one who wanted to go full steam ahead with that.'' Sienna glared at Cary.

Frowning, Cary asked, ''Are you saying this is all my fault?''

Jess interrupted them. ''It's not anybody's fault. I mean, it's not even a question of fault. Overall, we've been pretty successful, considering all we've tried to do. I just think we could do better.''

''It makes sense,'' Vivian agreed. ''What you're saying is we should map things out more, think ahead, plan for problems.''

Sienna nodded. ''I understand the part about using people's talents. I admit I hate collecting the cafeteria recyclables. I prefer the pet care hot line, talking to people.''

Ramon shook his head. "You can have it. I'm pretty sick of listening to people complain about Fluffy clawing the sofa or Fido's flea problem. I'd much rather collect cans."

"Well, Mr. Sanchez," said Mr. Montoya, "you may not enjoy giving information on the hot line, but I've noticed you're very good at *getting* information. Your talks with the school custodian really helped us in the beginning. Jess is absolutely right about each member having unique talents to contribute."

Sienna grinned. "I think I know what yours is, Cary. You're great at getting things going. Sometimes you go overboard, but from the very beginning of the Five Cat Club you've been the one with the most commitment."

Jess held her breath. Sienna seemed to be making a peace offering.

Cary shrugged. "Well, you're pretty good at certain things, too, like getting people interested in our group— television, newspapers . . ."

Deeply relieved, Jess marveled at what a switch it was for *her* to have played the peacemaker.

"So what do we do next?" Freedom asked. "We can't just sit around admiring each other."

Mr. Montoya chuckled. "Maybe it's better than the alternative we experienced earlier."

Laughing along with him, everyone seemed to have relaxed.

"I have a suggestion," said Mr. Montoya. "Sounds like you all agree on forming teams or committees to deal with the different projects. How about going ahead with that?"

"Yeah. That's how the SCMMA works." Ramon nodded.

Vivian started scribbling in her notebook. "We could have a school recycling committee and a neighborhood recycling committee. . . ."

"And another for the pet care hot line and animal issues," added Freedom. "Seems like the Five Cat Club's work has sort of fallen by the wayside lately. A separate committee for it might help rev it back up."

Jess sat back, listening to ideas fly around the room.

Ideas were still flying Friday at the first meeting of the neighborhood recycling team. The wind blew through the open garage door and brought the sharp, salty smell of the ocean into the headquarters.

During the past hour the new committee—composed of Jess, Cary, Ramon, and Webb—had been going over the whole recycling plan from start to finish. Because Buck's car was still dead and looked like it would stay that way until Buck could afford something like a heart transplant for it, they decided to count Buck and his car out forever. Instead, they would streamline the collection on foot. They'd borrow larger wheelbarrows, since those had proved best for hauling. They would outfit them with separate collection boxes for aluminum, plastic, and newspaper to keep things properly sorted along the way. No extra parents had volunteered to haul the stuff to the school on Saturdays, but Jess's father and Ms. Chen had agreed to continue helping on Sundays. And in an effort to quiet Mr. Wartman, the team would pile the recyclables in a spot farther back in the vacant lot, less in view of the street.

Jess leaned back in the old wooden chair, satisfied that things were finally shaping up for the Eco-kids' projects.

"Did you hear what the school recycling team is doing?" Ramon asked.

"I know they came up with a catchy name for themselves," said Cary. "The Recycling Royals, like the Jewel Beach Junior High Royals sports teams."

"Yup. Freedom said they decided they need lots of publicity and promotion to really get the idea of recycling into people's minds at school."

"If Sienna's on their team," interrupted Webb, "they won't have much trouble getting publicity."

"That's right," Ramon agreed. "She and her drama group are going to come up with some skits about recycling to put on during school assembly. Plus they got a bunch of ideas from that booklet that Mr. Montoya sent away for. Like, they're going to have a contest to see which classroom can gather the most white paper for recycling. And listen to this . . . they're putting on a dance."

"A dance?" Jess repeated.

"Yuck," said a voice in the kitchen doorway.

Luke stood there with Sam, who asked, "D'ya have to dance with girls?"

"Be quiet, you guys," Cary shushed them. "Nobody asked you."

Sam made a face. "Fine. We wouldn't want to go to some stupid dance anyway."

Jess agreed. She couldn't imagine dancing with any of the boys she knew. Maybe she wouldn't go, since she wasn't on the school recycling committee anyway. "How will a dance promote recycling?"

"I dunno," answered Ramon. "I guess they'll figure out a way."

The wind suddenly picked up and cycloned all the notes and papers around the table.

114

"Let's shut the garage door!" said Webb, rubbing his arms.

The temperature had dropped by several degrees in minutes, it seemed. Jess wondered if winter was finally coming, with Thanksgiving only a couple of weeks away.

"I'll shut it!" Sam insisted.

Just seconds after he pushed the button on the remote control box, Jess heard a squeal. Patti and Gina slipped in under the lowering door just in time.

"*Eee-eeh!* It almost got us!" Patti smoothed her dark hair.

"What're you guys doing?" asked Gina casually, glancing around.

"None of your beeswax," Sam told her.

"As a matter of fact, we're having some important discussions," said Jess. "So it's not a good time for you to be here."

"Yeah." Sam scowled at the two girls. "You kids scram."

"We mean *all* of you," Cary added.

Gina plopped into the beanbag chair, with Patti beside her. "We'll just listen."

"This is as much fun as wart removal," noted Ramon, but he was smiling. "Just stay quiet, kids, okay?"

The boys and girls nodded.

"You know," said Webb, "these committees were a great idea, but something just occurred to me. Last week we had tons of people working on the collection. This week we're only going to have four."

Ramon shrugged. "So it'll just take longer."

"The neighbors won't like that." Jess shook her head.

115

"Mr. Wartman is making enough of a fuss as it is," Cary added.

"Hey, how come we need more people?" Gina piped up from the beanbag chair, where she and Patti were petting Lucille.

"I thought you were going to listen *quietly*," said Jess.

"Well, yeah, but . . . how come?"

"The Eco-kids have split into different teams for different jobs," Ramon explained. "So now it's just us for the neighborhood recycling."

Webb ran a hand over his red hair. "There were always too many people before. Now there aren't enough."

"Why aren't eight people enough?" asked Patti.

"Eight?" Jess frowned, then realized what Patti meant. There were eight, counting herself and the other monkeys.

"You better let us help again," Sam warned.

Even Luke spoke up. "Remember how much we helped last time?"

"Hey, *we* helped the most," Gina shrieked. "Us girls."

"Quiet down, folks," Ramon told them calmly.

"Well?" Patti whispered. "Can we still help?"

"The way you kids behave, 'help' is not the word," said Cary.

"Anyway, we're talking about the number of actual people we'll have available," Webb explained politely.

"*We're* people. *We're* actual people," insisted Gina.

"He means actual *older* people," Jess told her. "People like us." She was trying to be polite, too, but she could hear the better-than-you tone in her own voice.

116

Luke frowned.

Then Ramon tried. "Members. We're talking about the number of *members* of our club that we need to help."

"Why can't we be members?" Sam demanded.

Exasperated, Jess realized that Ramon had just opened a can of worms.

Patti jumped on the bandwagon. "Yeah. We've helped as much as anyone. Maybe more."

"More than the boys, that's for sure," muttered Gina.

"You stupid bimbo!" Sam started across the room toward her.

Ramon shot an arm out and snagged him just in time.

"See, this is why we don't want you kids around." Cary pointed her finger at them. "You're always getting into fights."

"*They* start it," countered Gina. "The boys bug us!"

Jess shook her head. "It doesn't matter who starts it. The problem is that *we* end up having to finish it. We don't have time for this."

"That's not the kind of member we need in our club," added Webb.

"But you *do* need us!" Patti cried. "Don't you remember how much we helped, especially that first recycling day?"

"Yeah, you were about to give up when we came to the rescue with our trucks and doll buggies." Gina puffed herself up proudly.

The boys on the other side of the room rolled their eyes, but didn't argue.

"You can't say you weren't glad to have us around," Luke added.

All the kids looked earnest and anxious, Jess noticed,

as if they couldn't bear to be left out. They wanted so badly to be accepted. Suddenly it hit Jess: that was probably how she herself looked around her sister. She knew how awful it felt to be ignored, talked down to, brushed off.

And she had to admit that the kids were right about one thing. They *had* been helpful.

Webb echoed her thoughts. "Well, it's true that they helped as much as anyone."

"Yeah, in between their spats they can be good workers," Cary noted.

Jess saw a look pass between the girls' and the boys' side of the room.

"Listen, we promise we'll stop fighting," Gina offered. "Right, guys?"

Luke shrugged. "Sure."

Jess chuckled. "Luke, that promise means nothing from you, because you never fight with them, anyway. It's mostly Matt. Sam is runner up."

"And Matt isn't here to promise." Cary pointed out. "Can you guys make him behave?"

"Yeah, and how about if you girls just ignore them," suggested Ramon. "Be cool, okay?"

The girls looked at each other and nodded.

"We'll ignore them," Patti promised eagerly.

"Aw, calm down." Sam waved his hand at the girls. "We couldn't care less about you. We won't come anywhere near you. Matt won't, neither."

"Promise?" asked Ramon.

Sam held up his hand and hoisted up Luke's, too, in a scout salute.

"Scout's honor," they vowed.

Ramon grinned. "Good enough for me."

118

Jess followed Sam and his wheelbarrow down Opal Street. They stopped at Mrs. Kiplinger's to load up her newspapers, then went on to the Farmers' box full of cans and bottles next door. Farther along, Webb and his helpers, Patti and Gina, worked on the Sykes family's piles of plastic soda bottles. The other teams, Ramon with Matt, and Cary with her brother Luke, had taken Emerald Drive and Ruby Lane as part of the new, improved recycling plan.

Just days before Thanksgiving, it was the warmest Saturday all fall. The week's earlier cold front had blown right through and away. Now a yellow beach ball of a sun made everything feel like summer.

Mopping her forehead with a shirt sleeve, Jess glanced at the watch on her wrist. Only one o'clock. Whether it was the sunshine, the new plan and "mini-team" strategy, or some combination of them all that had made the day go so well, she couldn't say. But the fact was that in only one hour the teams had swept through nearly the whole neighborhood, gathering mountains of recyclables in the vacant lot.

"Hi, kids." Penny Allbright waved at Jess's team from the flower bed she was weeding. She got up and brushed the dirt off her tie-dyed sundress, walking toward them with clogs thunking on her flagstone path. "How's it going?"

"Great, Ms. Allbright," said Sam. "We've got lots of stuff."

"Call me Penny." She smiled and pushed her long brown braid over a shoulder. "Congratulations on the great job you're doing. It was high time we started recycling in this neighborhood."

"We think so, too," Jess agreed.

Penny leaned her elbows on the top of her wooden fence. "It's neat that you're using foot power for the collection instead of a car now. Better for the environment probably, huh?"

Jess shrugged, wondering whether or not to admit that they hadn't thought of that.

Meanwhile, Sam nodded proudly. "Yeah, we're saving the environment."

Jess couldn't believe her ears. She'd had no idea that the little kids were at all interested in the club's real purpose. She did a double take at Sam. All along it had seemed that he and the others were just participating for the fun of it or to be in on something with the "big kids." How amazing that Sam should say such a thing!

Waving good-bye to Penny, the two of them headed for the vacant lot to dump the full wheelbarrow.

"After this we'll just have one trip left," Sam told Jess. "Just three more houses."

They passed Joel Sobieski in his front yard playing stickball with his toddlers Kimmie and Jason.

"Hi, Mr. Sobieski!" called Sam.

Mr. Sobieski waved just before Jason tripped over a rock and landed on his chin.

Unharmed and gently comforted by his father, Jason nevertheless wailed loud enough to make Sam cover his ears. The scene gave Jess an astonishing thought. Maybe she was looking at future Eco-kids. Eventually she and Cary and the others would probably leave Opal Street to go to college. Sam might someday take her place in the club. And then someday Kimmie and Jason might follow Sam and his pals. Maybe taking the younger kids into the neighborhood recycling team hadn't been such a bad idea. After all, it was one way to spread the word about the earth and the environment to a younger generation.

Approaching the vacant lot, Jess was even more shocked to see that Mr. Wartman had actually come down from his balcony.

He pointed at the recycling piles. "How long are you going to leave that back there? It's an eyesore. It attracts vermin."

"What's vermin?" asked Ramon. Wearing rubber gloves, he and Matt were sorting the bottles, cans, and newspapers.

"Don't sass me, young man. You know very well what I mean. Rats. Bugs. This neighborhood will be overrun by them, you'll see, if this keeps up."

Jess noticed Sam, wide-eyed, draw close to her side. Mr. Wartman was quite a sight. His gray hair stuck out all around like Bert's on *Sesame Street*. Very tall, he wore blue Bermuda shorts, a white undershirt, black socks and black dress shoes, and a constant frown.

Jess gathered her courage. "Hello, Mr. Wartman. Is there a problem?"

Mr. Wartman snorted. "Hah! Is there a problem, she asks. The ridiculous notions you children get. Rebicy-

121

cling, whatever you call it. That's the problem! Turning the neighborhood into a garbage dump every Saturday.''

"Recycling," Jess corrected.

"Don't sass me. I'm going to city hall about this. Just you wait. They'll put a stop to this nonsense.''

"You can't do that!" cried Matt.

"Oh? Can't I?"

Jess heard the *thunk-thunk* of clogs on the sidewalk.

"No, sir," answered Penny Allbright, "in fact, you can't.''

Startled, Mr. Wartman turned to look at Penny.

"The neighborhood wants and needs recycling, Mr. Wartman. It's good for all of us, even *you*," she said.

"Hmph! Now they're trying to tell me what's good for me. Just who do you think you are?''

"My name is Penny. I live across the street there. No disrespect intended, Mr. Wartman. It's just that what I hear from the other neighbors is nothing but praise for this group of kids.''

Drawing himself up to his full height, Mr. Wartman pointed at his house. "Mrs. Wartman and I moved into this neighborhood in 1967. We plan to—" He stopped and cleared his throat. "*I* plan to stay.''

Jess noticed something sad in his eyes.

"You young ones come and go," he went on. "Meanwhile, you have no respect for peace and quiet, for order and neighborhood pride. Make a big mess and expect the rest of us to look at it every day.''

"Not every day," Sam offered meekly, "just one day.''

Mr. Wartman turned the full force of his glare on him. "I don't care if it's one day or one hour!''

Sam shrank back. So did Jess. To be yelled at in

public was terribly embarrassing. She hoped her father wouldn't hear. No doubt he'd come out, soothe Mr. Wartman, then scold the Eco-kids again about annoying the neighbors. As if it were their fault that Mr. Wartman was such a grump!

As it was, the spectacle had already attracted Penny. Now, out of the corner of her eye Jess saw Mr. Sobieski and his kids approaching.

He strolled up, toting little Jason in his arms and pulling Kimmie by the hand. "Hi," he said, chuckling. "What's all the commotion over here?"

"It's no laughing matter, Joel!" Mr. Wartman informed him. "I want you to stop these children. You live right next door to this mess they're creating."

Mr. Sobieski shrugged. "I guess I don't see it as a mess, Mr. Wartman. It's lowering everyone's garbage bill."

Although Mr. Wartman was still frowning, Jess caught a flicker of interest in his eyes. But he covered it up by saying, "*Hmph!* At the expense of our home values! This neighborhood is going to ruin, mark my words!"

Penny shook her head. "On the contrary. Most people nowadays see recycling as a plus—a positive point for living in a neighborhood. And most people like the idea of the community involvement it brings, too. Residents take more of an interest in their neighborhood, in each other. . . ."

"Call it any kind of fancy name you want, but it still comes down to that garbage dump right on my own street!" Mr. Wartman pointed accusingly at the collection mounds.

"So, your complaint," said Mr. Sobieski, repositioning Jason on his hip, "is about this." He pointed at the piles, too.

"Sitting here all day, all night, attracting vermin . . ." Mr. Wartman grumbled.

"It has to sit here, because we don't have transportation to our school dump until Sunday," Jess explained.

"Really?" asked Penny. "Is that the problem?"

Mr. Sobieski shook his head. "That's not much of a problem. Someone could help out. My wife, for instance, brings the car back at two today."

Penny smiled at Jess and Ramon. "Why didn't you say something earlier? I told you I'd be happy to help."

"Hey, you'll drive us?" asked Ramon.

"My pickup is a bit battered," she replied, "but it runs fine."

"Hi!" called Gina, pushing a cart toward them.

Not far behind came Webb with Patti and a wheelbarrow.

Mr. Wartman took one look at the newspapers in Gina's cart and the jumble of bottles and cans in the wheelbarrow. He squinted his eyes and wrinkled his nose.

"Don't worry, Mr. Wartman." Jess tried to sound reassuring like her father. "It will all be gone very soon."

He grunted, spun on a heel, and marched back to his house.

The second the old man's back was turned, Ramon leapt into the air with both fists high. "Yes!"

Webb, Matt, Mr. Sobieski, and Penny joined him in high-fives. But from the frustrated look Jess had seen on Mr. Wartman's face, she got the distinct feeling that they hadn't heard the last from him.

*　*　*

Cary leaned back on her elbows and sighed. "This sure beats hauling garbage."

She and Jess lounged in the knee-high grass on China Hill Sunday afternoon, watching for whales out on the glossy blue Pacific. The highest point in Jewel Beach, the hill had gotten its name for its wide, clear views of the ocean, San Diego and, in some people's imaginations, even China.

"It's definitely great to get the neighborhood recycling done in one day, rather than having it carry over to Sunday," Jess added. "I hated having to rush through Sunday dinner and pull on those wonderful rubber gloves."

"Thanks to Penny and Mr. Sobieski helping us out." Cary nodded. "Why didn't we think of asking them sooner? I mean, it makes perfect sense to ask neighbors for help on neighborhood recycling, right?"

Jess picked a dandelion. "I think there are some things we just have to learn as we go on these projects. They're not going to start off perfectly."

Cary nodded. "That's for sure."

Cary's dogs, Bal and Lucille, flew by in pursuit of a black Labrador retriever carrying a stick. The dogs dashed all around the small hillside meadow, politely avoiding the families picnicking and the group of teenagers playing hacky-sack. They did, however, upset a snuggly couple at the meadow's edge when Bal's tail smacked the man in the face. The man turned and glared at the girls.

"Bal! Lucille!" Cary ran after them. "Come play over here."

After rounding up the dogs, Cary sat down again,

125

biting her lip. "How embarrassing. Speaking of embarrassment . . . Jess, would you answer a question? Honestly, I mean. Promise you'll be honest."

"Of course. About what?"

"Well, you and I have been friends for a long time. It's up to friends to tell friends things, right?"

"What things?" asked Jess. "Out with it, Cary."

Cary shrugged. "Well . . . am I . . . am I a jerk?"

Jess couldn't help it—she had to laugh. "That's pretty straightforward."

"But really, am I? All those things Ramon and Freedom and Vivian were saying during the meeting. About my being . . . a pain and everything. I guess I was, wasn't I?"

Jess looked at her, wondering what to say. The last thing she wanted to do was hurt her friend's feelings, but she had promised to be honest. "You're no jerk, Cary. Sometimes, when you get impatient with us, it's hard to understand why. And—" Jess took a breath—here was the hardest part. "And I guess I have to admit that a couple of times I felt sort of well, hurt."

"How come?"

Jess shrugged. "Sometimes you're off in another world. I mean, as far as our friendship goes."

"You mean, I don't pay attention to you?" Cary frowned in concern.

"You've been pretty focused on club stuff lately."

Cary nodded. "I sure didn't mean to ignore you."

"I didn't think you meant to," Jess reassured her.

"Listen, Jess." Cary hugged her knees. "Next time I get too focused on club stuff, just shake me out of it, okay?"

Jess laughed. "Okay."

126

"Jess?"

"Hmm?"

Cary sighed. "What I mean is . . . I'm really glad you're my friend."

"Me, too," Jess answered.

"I mean, I want it to stay that way." Cary bit her lip.

Jess nodded. "Me, too."

They exchanged relieved smiles.

If only it were so easy to work out all problems. Like the one with Beth. Inside, Jess felt almost like two people. Half of her couldn't stand her sister. The other half longed for their friendship back.

Bal galumphed over and planted his huge paws in Jess's lap, demanding her attention. Only six months old, he had already outgrown older Lucille by about a foot. Jess scratched behind his gold-brown ears. It was hard to believe that just a few months ago he had been a scruffy little puppy left in a box at the Chens' front door.

"Don't you think he looks like a German shepherd?" asked Cary.

"Yes," Jess replied, "if you crossed one with a bear."

Bal gave her a long lick from chin to forehead.

"Oh, thanks!" She wiped her face with a shirt sleeve. "His behavior, however, is strictly puppy."

He flopped over on his back to plead forgiveness. Not to be left out, Lucille left her Labrador pal and crowded between the girls for some attention.

Cary sighed contentedly. "Isn't this just the best? Great dogs, great weather, nothin' to do . . ."

Jess nodded. Maybe this is what they'd both been needing—a lazy day off from club work, schoolwork,

127

and everything else. She gazed down at the golden beach footing the hillside. A shallow stream cut through the sand, spouting from a natural spring somewhere near the hill bottom and fanning out into the ocean. Shorebirds tittered about at the surf's edge. A little farther out, a line of a half-dozen brown pelicans glided low over the white-foamed breakers. Surfers bobbed on their boards waiting for bigger waves.

"See any whales yet?" asked Cary.

Jess shook her head. "It's still a little early in the season. The California gray whales migrate all the way down from the Arctic Circle in mid-autumn. They're just beginning to arrive in southern California now."

"And they're headed for Mexico, right?" asked Cary.

"The part called Baja California." Jess nodded. "Or 'lower California.' The lagoon waters are warm there, so they can have their babies. Then in February they start migrating back north."

"Why not just stay in the south?" Cary wondered. "I mean since they're even called *California* gray whales."

"Food, probably. Their main supply seems to be in the colder waters."

"They eat a lot, don't they?"

Jess laughed. "Tons. Small fish and tiny shrimptype creatures and microorganisms. In bulk."

"Mmm. Delicious." Cary leaned her head to the side. "I like to think that maybe we're helping them."

"Who?" asked Jess. "The whales?"

Cary nodded. "A little. I mean, they almost went extinct a few years ago because of people hunting them. Well, recycling helps keep the ocean just a little bit cleaner for them, with less toxic waste and stuff. Maybe we can help keep them from almost going extinct again.''

''I hope so,'' Jess agreed. ''Maybe the Eco-kids haven't done everything you hoped we would, but at least we've—'' She interrupted herself and pointed out to sea. ''Oh, look!''

Beyond the surfers, the spray from a whale's spout hovered in a tall column above the water.

''Wow!'' cried Cary.

Everyone in the meadow, including the dogs, stopped to look.

Another spout came up right behind the first, then another to the side.

''It's a whole herd!'' someone said.

''Pod,'' Cary whispered, ''a group of them is called a pod, right?''

Jess nodded, too enthralled to speak.

She counted five clouds of mist clinging to the ocean's surface, amazed at the fact that she was seeing the condensation from the whales' exhaled breaths. Suspended for only moments in the soft afternoon light, the spouts were dreamily beautiful, and as temporary as rainbows.

''You want me to *what?*'' Jess frowned at Ramon over the top of her glasses.

''Dance with me. Come on. It's not such a big deal.''

''Not a big deal? You won't even sit at our lunch table and you're asking me to *dance* with you?''

Ramon shrugged. ''Sitting together at lunch is different. But you're *supposed* to dance at a dance.''

Behind him, on the floor of the school gym, lots of people were indeed dancing. Most of them were eighth graders, but a few seventh graders hit the dance floor, too. It was a great turnout for the Can Do Dance, as the school recycling committee had called it in the announcements and on the posters all over Jewel Beach Junior High.

Jess decided to ignore Ramon. Maybe he'd go away. She had agreed to attend the dance in case the school recycling team, the Recycling Royals, needed extra help. She had *not* come to dance.

In the doorway nearby, Freedom and Vivian took the soda cans that people brought as admission to the Can Do. Ten aluminum cans equalled a ticket, or five cans and one dollar. They had gotten the idea from the booklet about recycling that Mr. Montoya had sent for. Meanwhile, as the official dance hostess, Sienna wandered around talking to people, introducing them to each other, making sure there were no wallflowers. Apparently she was doing a good job, because no one looked bored.

In fact everything seemed to be under control. In a corner near the stage the newest Eco-kids, Hallie Greer and Derek Han, ran the refreshments table. Mr. Montoya and Ms. Toshimi the English teacher acted as the faculty chaperones. The gym looked great, festooned with garlands made from recyclable white paper and newspaper. On the walls hung a couple of the posters of Leon and Tamara and a mural-sized photo of Earth as seen from the moon. Vivian and Hallie had made a gigantic mobile out of saved-up Popsicle sticks, kite string, and dozens of soda cans and plastic bottles. It turned and twisted on a rafter at the very center of the dance floor, catching the light as a colorful, floor-to-ceiling Eco-kids Christmas tree.

"Hi, Jess! Don't just stand there! Come on and dance!" This time it was Sienna, not Ramon.

Jess shook her head. "I never said I'd dance. I'm here to help."

"Oh, don't be such a wet rag. We don't need help right now. We need everyone to dance and have a good time." Sienna grabbed her arm.

"Hey!" Jess protested.

"Come on! Loosen up! Let's party!"

Jess dug in her heels and tried to get her arm back, but she was in the grip of a girl on a mission. Before she could get away Sienna had dragged her out near the "tree." In its sparky reflections Sienna moved right into a funky dance step.

Jess wanted to disappear. She didn't mind dancing at home and at family parties, but out in public? It was embarrassing. She made a few moves anyway to satisfy her friend. Fortunately Sienna's attention span was short. Soon she'd wander off to bother someone else and Jess could sneak away. But before that could happen Ramon sauntered up and joined in, performing like someone in a rock video. Together he and Sienna could have been on MTV. Ramon would do something and Sienna would pick it up. Or she would make a move and he would follow.

Jess shook her head in amazement. She had seen Sienna practice her dance routines before, and once in a while Ramon would do something spontaneous like a floor spin, but never like this. Soon the floor cleared and the other dancers gathered around to watch.

"Hey, what's that move, Sienna?" someone called to her.

A rap song had come on the tape, and Sienna was

wiggling through some cross between a Roger Rabbit and a moon walk.

"Yeah, whaddya call this, Sabo?" Ramon yelled over the music, trying to keep up with her.

Smiling, Sienna shrugged.

From his spot at the door, Freedom yelled out, "It's the Recycle Rap!"

That seemed to inspire Ramon. He started singing. " 'The toe bone's connected with the . . . foot bone . . .' " It was the same ditty he had come up with a few weeks before, now set to the rap song on the tape.

Sienna laughed and joined in. Within a few seconds, other people were singing along, too.

"The river's connected with the . . . ocean . . . The ocean's connected with the . . . raindrop . . ."

Jess couldn't believe her ears—or her eyes. People were starting to imitate Sienna's shimmies and slides.

"That's it!" Sienna encouraged them. "Everybody now, move it! That's right. Now roll it."

On all sides, Jess was surrounded by schoolmates rapping and rolling. It looked stupid. It sounded even stupider, the lyrics making little sense at all. However, she had to admit, it did look like fun.

She really couldn't help herself. She had started to mouth the ridiculous words and shimmy and slide with the rest.

At one point, everyone shook their hands above their heads and clapped twice. Jess heard her own voice sing out as loud as anyone's. "We're doin' the Ree, doin' the Ree, doin' the Ree-cycle Rap!"

11

"We're going to be on TV!"

Sienna burst into the classroom a few seconds before 8 A.M., gesturing wildly, eyes bright. Cary followed behind her, looking a little dazed.

"Who's 'we'?" asked Jess. The girls had walked to school together but Sienna took so long at her locker that Jess had gone on to first period alone.

"The Eco-kids!" Sienna answered. "Channel Six heard about the Can Do Dance because Erin Manning-Bishop's mother works at the station and her mother told the news department and they told Freddy Fredemeyer and he's coming out today!"

"How did you learn about this?" asked Ms. Toshimi.

"The school secretary just told Sienna," Cary explained. "They've got the idea that she's the Eco-kids president."

"That's 'cause she's always talking," Derek Han put in.

"Well, I am not the president," corrected Sienna. "We don't even have officers. Just committees and committee leaders and chairpersons. And I happen to be the Recycling Royals' publicity leader, so it's just as well he told *me*." She buffed her fingernails on her lapel.

"Well, then," said Ms. Toshimi, "what's your plan?"

Sienna frowned. "For what?"

The teacher smiled. "The reporter's visit. What are you going to say to Freddy Fredemeyer?"

"The usual, I guess." Sienna shrugged. "Just explain stuff."

"Well, I suggest you give it some thought first," Ms. Toshimi responded.

Before she could elaborate, Mr. Gormley came on the loudspeaker with his laundry list of daily announcements—pep rally at 2 P.M., no loitering outside the convenience store across the street, all-school assembly next Tuesday morning. When he finished Ms. Toshimi picked up where she had left off.

"Communication is a powerful tool. And in this case, your form of communication will be television. It gives you an opportunity to show yourself in the light in which you want to be seen and to help other people understand your ideas and goals. Freddy Fredemeyer's report is going to be watched by thousands of TV viewers. What do you want them to see and hear about the Eco-kids?"

"Everything," Cary answered.

"That's the problem." Ms. Toshimi shook her head. "You usually don't have time to explain everything, so you should be prepared with the most important messages and images you want people to take away with them." She tapped a finger on her desk. "In fact, I think I'm going to change the plan for today's class. Television is very important in our culture. It shapes our perspectives and opinions, has a big influence on our lives. Let's spend this hour talking about how *we,*

134

for once, can turn around and make the influence on others.''

Not one of Jess's favorite subjects, English sometimes got boring. But not that day. Everyone jumped into the discussion. Before the hour was over they had come up with a plan for the Eco-kids' appearance on TV.

''And in this alcove we have our cafeteria recycling center.'' Mr. Gormley grinned broadly at the Channel Six camera, rocking back and forth on his heels. He waved an arm at the boxes for aluminum and plastic, taking them in as if they belonged to him.

Standing beside him with some of the other club members, Jess stared in wonder. She had never seen the principal smile before. And certainly never seen him smile at the recycling boxes.

''We're doing a pretty good job here,'' Mr. Gormley told the reporter. His white shirt buttoned tightly over his belly, and his tie knot fit snug under his Adam's apple. ''We feel it's a service to the community, as well as to our school. Recycling is something we feel strongly about.''

Jess and Cary exchanged glances.

Ramon hissed, *''We?''*

Sienna said, ''It certainly is something we feel strongly about.''

The camera swung on her.

Like a candle just lit, she flickered to life, her face aglow with the pleasure of being on stage. ''We Eco-kids believe that if everyone does his or her part, we can make a difference.''

Before she could continue with the list of important points they'd worked out in English class, Mr. Gormley

135

clapped her on the back. "Exactly. Make a difference. That's what we do here at Jewel Beach Junior High. We aim to—"

"How exactly did you kids get started on this project?" the reporter Freddy Fredemeyer interrupted. He wore his trademark bow tie, today in red.

The camera stayed on Sienna. She told the story and went on to describe the neighborhood recycling project, too. A couple of times Mr. Gormley broke in to say that the Jewel Beach Junior High faculty and administration had encouraged "these youngsters" every step of the way.

Freddy ignored him. The camera focused on Sienna, and when she was finished it turned to Ramon.

"What's your reason for being an Eco-kid?" Freddy asked him.

As a warning not to get cute, Cary poked Ramon in the ribs.

He poked Cary back, then told the camera, "Well, somebody's got to do something. Us kids, we might be young and all, but we do a lot. I like the Eco-kids because it makes me feel like I can get stuff done. Help fix stuff."

Freddy smiled. "Fantastic." He turned to Jess. "And *your* reason for joining the Eco-kids?"

"Mine?" She swallowed and stammered. "I—uh . . ." Then she remembered the issues they had discussed in class that morning. "The earth," she managed to say, gathering courage. "It's our home. The only one we've got. I want to keep it a nice place to live."

"Beautifully put." Freddy Fredemeyer nodded. "Who could ask for more from this great bunch of young people? The city of Jewel Beach is indeed fortunate to have among its citizenry such forward-looking youths.'' He smiled. ''Congratulations to all of you, and keep up the good work.''

When he started to sign off, Mr. Gormley sidled up beside him.

''For Channel Six news,'' said Freddy, ''this is . . .''

Mr. Gormley grinned widely at the camera.

''Freddy Fredemeyer, at—''

''Jewel Beach Junior High,'' Mr. Gormley finished for him, waving at the camera like a little boy.

Jess had one eye on the TV and one eye on her parents and grandmother that evening when the story came on the news. She wasn't sure who was more astonished, her or them, to see what a big news item the Eco-kids had become.

The station aired not only Freddy Fredemeyer's report from their school but also several interviews with city officials where Freddy asked them why it was left up to kids to start recycling programs.

''Why doesn't the city offer curbside recycling services to its residents, along with garbage pickup?'' he demanded. ''Kids shouldn't have to this, should they?''

The mayor murmured and stammered something about looking into the proposal. The police chief said it might cause traffic problems and health hazards. Freddy went on to talk with leaders of local environmental groups who said they'd been trying for years to get city-wide recycling.

''Well, with these Eco-kids in the picture,'' said one of the leaders, ''maybe Jewel Beach will finally wake up and demand this essential service that so many other cities enjoy.''

137

When the report ended, the news anchorwoman followed up with, "Join us at noon tomorrow for a visit to the Eco-kids' neighborhood recycling project."

"Goodness!" exclaimed Jess's mother.

Dad shook his head. "You kids are really something."

"Your club certainly is kicking up a fuss, isn't it?" Grammy grinned. "Getting all these government folks worked up about how shameful they look, leaving it up to children to do their dirty work."

Dad shook his head, smiling at the same time. "You are causing a citywide controversy, you know?"

"Well, no one's more surprised than me," Jess confessed. "Freddy didn't tell us about coming out here tomorrow! I'd better call Cary. I had no idea!"

On her way to the hall phone she was so preoccupied that she almost ran smack into Beth in the doorway.

Beth's arms were crossed. Her eyes fixed on her sister.

Jess might have gone around her, but hesitated. This was the closest to any sort of communication that she and Beth had come in weeks.

For a second their eyes met, then Beth leaned against the doorframe to let Jess pass.

Jess took a breath and walked by. She had gone no further than a few steps when she realized she was being followed.

Acting nonchalant, Beth stopped when Jess did.

It was an odd sort of dance. Jess decided to end it. "Do you want something?"

Beth shrugged. "Was that you on TV?"

"With my club." Jess nodded. "The Eco-kids. A

138

reporter came to our school to cover our recycling program.''

''Oh. Sounds interesting.''

Jess couldn't think of what to say. ''It is,'' was all that came out.

All her defenses were up. She didn't trust her sister as far as she could throw her. Any second Beth might come up with something cold and cutting or just walk away and leave her dangling—the kid sister she didn't want to hang around with anymore.

At the same time, though, Jess's heart ached for the way things used to be. She wished that somehow Beth wold finally break down with an apology. *I've been a really rotten person,* she would say, *and I'm awfully sorry. Be my friend again.*

Instead, Beth just said, ''Congratulations.''

Jess squinted. ''For what?''

''Your club. Being on TV. All the stuff you've been doing. It's impressive.''

Jess knew she should be polite and just accept the praise, but her mouth went off in another direction. ''You mean now that I've been on TV you feel I'm worth your attention?''

''That's a lousy attitude, Jess.''

''So is yours.''

''Look, I just wanted to congratulate you. If you can't accept that—''

''Don't pin this on me,'' Jess spat out. ''You haven't spoken to me in a month.''

''Well, what about *you?*'' Beth recrossed her arms. ''I haven't heard you knocking on *my* door.''

''Oh, right. So I could get it slammed in my face?

139

I don't think so. You haven't wanted anything to do with me.''

"How ridiculous!'' Beth made a disgusted face.

"Did you or did you not tell me I was just a kid?'' Jess demanded. "And that you couldn't hang around with me anymore?''

Finally caught out, Beth sputtered, "Well, you just took it too hard. I didn't mean I didn't want to spend *any* time with you.''

"How much time am I allowed then, your royal highness?''

"Oh, cut the sarcasm.'' Beth wrinkled her nose. "Try to listen for once, okay?''

"It's not much fun to listen to people who cut you down.'' Jess crossed her arms angrily.

"I never meant to cut you down, Jess. I—I see I hurt your feelings. And . . . I'm sorry.''

Jess eyed her suspiciously.

Beth looked right back into her eyes. "I really am. We misunderstood each other. I didn't think about how what I said to you would sound.''

Jess waited, feeling her guard start to come down, just an inch.

Beth shook her head. "Everything I said must have sounded like a rejection of you. But see, soon after I got home from New York I started wishing I was already finished with high school and could go out and start painting more seriously. I've been feeling like I need independence. Maybe I should have explained that to you instead of saying what I did. I need more space from Mama and Dad and Grammy, and even from you, sometimes.''

Busy processing it all, Jess didn't want to say any-

140

thing yet. She didn't want her sister to get the idea that all was forgiven. Curiosity, though, finally got the better of her. "How would you support yourself out on your own?"

Beth laughed. "That *would* be a problem. I'm not saying it's what I want to do—go off and be on my own. It's just how I feel these days. Sometimes being alone with my own friends helps."

"So I'm supposed to not take it personally," Jess said dryly.

"Exactly," agreed her sister.

Jess sighed and shook her head. "Is this like one of those things Sienna is always talking about?"

"Which things?" Beth frowned quizzically.

"All that pop psychology mumbo jumbo she comes up with. Like the phases of adolescence or whatever."

Beth shrugged. This time Jess could tell it was a genuine shrug and not the arrogant, stuck-up kind. "Could be. Anyway, I've been painting it out."

"What do you mean? Putting your feelings into your paintings?"

Beth nodded. "I've never tried it before. I mean, not intentionally."

"Sounds depressing. Sitting there mulling over your worries while you paint . . ." Jess made a face.

"Well, what do you do with *your* worries?" her sister asked.

The question took Jess aback. What *did* she do with them? What had she been doing with her worries over Beth all those weeks? In the beginning she had held them in. Then Grammy had made her talk and think about the problem. That had given her some practice so that when she talked with Cary about *their* disagreements, she was able to express herself better.

"I guess I'm slowly learning what to do," she answered her sister.

Beth leaned against the wall. "That makes two of us."

Just then Mama started to come out of the den into the hallway. She looked up and saw her daughters standing together. The look on her face was priceless. Like a car backing up, she quickly threw herself into reverse and hurried in the other direction, nearly stumbling over the doorstep.

Beyond the doorway, Jess spotted Grammy and Dad craning their necks toward the sight of the two girls talking for the first time in weeks.

The sight of *them* made Jess and her sister double over and crack up laughing.

In the merriment, Beth set askew one of her paintings on the wall behind her. An older one, of a bowl of fruit on a wooden table, it was easy to understand. Back in the days when she had painted it, Beth was easy to understand, too. But like her newer paintings, Beth wasn't so easy to understand anymore. She was moving on, changing.

It occurred to Jess that Beth wasn't the only one moving on. Over the past few months she herself had changed a lot, too.

Change made life seem very hard. Very confusing.

She looked at her sister, who was knuckling tears away from her eyes after that good, hard laugh.

Change could be a bother, but she had to admit, it certainly kept life interesting.

Life got even more interesting on Saturday morning.

Two dozen people jammed into the Chens' garage, many of them attending their first-ever Eco-kids meeting. Sienna was in top form, meeting and greeting the new arrivals. Cary passed out sheets of information about the club.

After the Channel Six report, the Jewel Beach Junior High offices and the pet care hot line had been swamped with calls from kids all over town wanting to join. A general meeting before the neighborhood recycling pickup seemed like the best way to welcome the new members.

When everyone was settled in, Sienna said, "Freddy Fredemeyer won't be here till noon. Why don't we introduce ourselves and say why we're here?"

A new girl with glasses and a long black braid started off. "I'm Sheela Chopra. I'm in sixth grade at Jewel Beach Elementary. I love animals. I want to help them."

The next girl said, "Well, I go to Jewel Beach Junior High and I knew about the Eco-kids already, but when I saw you on TV I thought it looked really cool and fun, you know, plus I like nature and everything. I like hiking and camping up in the mountains with my parents, and I want there to be places like that left when I grow up. Oh, and my name is Kristin Capelli."

"Yeah," added a boy Jess recognized from her church. "I want there to be a clean ocean left when I grow up. I'm a surfer. Name's Nate Mackey."

Jess spotted the Eco-juniors on the other side of the room. None of them had made a sound yet. They seemed amazed by the crowd. So was she. She'd never imagined that other kids around the city would be interested in environmental issues—enough to join their club. Nor could she have imagined being on TV twice in one week. Freddy Fredemeyer and his crew would be arriving at noon to cover neighborhood recycling day.

Kristin asked, ''I see the different committees on this sheet you gave us. Are we supposed to choose one to be on?''

''Sure.'' Ramon nodded. ''One, two, three, as many as you want.''

''Well, that's true,'' Webb agreed, ''but not many of us have time for more than one or two at the most.''

Cary sat forward. ''Right. We all need to remember that we're not just 'on' a committee. We *work* on the committee. This is a working club. I mean, we try to get things done.''

''Yeah, watch out,'' warned Ramon, grinning. ''If you don't work hard enough Cary'll nail you.''

A couple of the new members glanced at her warily.

''Aw, just joking. She's not so bad,'' Ramon reassured them.

Cary sat back and shook her head. ''But if you don't watch out for *him* he'll drive you batty!''

Ramon crossed his eyes, flapped his arms, wiggled his ears, and screeched like a bat all at the same time.

Everyone, including Cary, burst out laughing. Jess felt relieved that the Eco-kids could chuckle about their past disagreements. They had made a lot of progress since that day when Freedom inspected their lunch trash. She, for one, now knew the answers to a few of the questions she'd had before. How to get along better with others. How to be honest with your feelings and express them to prevent misunderstandings. And most important, like Grammy said, you didn't need to change yourself to please people, as long as you were true to your own heart.

At about a quarter to twelve a white van pulled up to the curb in front of the Chens' house. On its doors it bore the big blue Channel Six logo and on top it sported a satellite dish and a tangle of wires.

"We're going *live!*" called Freddy Fredemeyer, sprinting up the driveway. "They've scheduled us on the noon news." Today he wore a blue bow tie with little cat faces on it. "Ready to show me around before we go on? We've got twenty-five minutes."

Eco-kids and Eco-juniors old and new abandoned the meeting. Some rushed over to inspect the news van, and the rest led Freddy and the camerawoman through the headquarters. They leafed through the pamphlets for the pet care hot line and checked out the posters on the walls.

"Hah! I like that one!" remarked the camerawoman, pointing at a photo of the earth. The caption read LOVE YOUR MOTHER.

Next they visited the vacant lot next door. Sienna explained that it was where the club had gotten started, that day last summer when she and Jess and Cary had found the kittens in a trash heap.

"This is your collection area, right?" asked Freddy. "Well, I know you don't begin your recycling pickup till one o'clock, but we've got to air our report in—" He glanced at his watch. "Six minutes. Could some of you start the collection a little early for me?"

Webb and some of the others moved off to oblige.

Then, suddenly, Matt yelled, "Hi, Mr. Wartman!" He waved up at the old man on his balcony.

Jess swallowed. Wonderful. Just what they needed.

145

Mr. Wartman on TV with them. At least the camera wasn't rolling yet.

No sooner had she finished the thought than the camerawoman aimed at him.

"Good idea. Let's get some filler for the evening news," Freddy told her.

Mr. Wartman spotted the camera and started to scurry inside.

Freddy called, "Hi there! Freddy Fredemeyer with Channel Six. How are you, sir?"

Mr. Wartman turned back and stared down suspiciously, a warlord defending his castle.

"Hello!" Freddy yelled louder. "Quite a group of young folks in your neighborhood, isn't there? You're on camera, sir. Anything you'd like to say?"

Wonderful, just wonderful. Jess wrung her hands. Mr. Wartman would probably not present the Eco-kids in the best light, as Ms. Toshimi would say.

She heard a muffled cough from the balcony.

"Did you see them on TV the other night?" Freddy asked. "See their recycling project in school? Now you've got one right here!"

Jess held her breath. Cary, Sienna, and Ramon, who all knew Mr. Wartman, were doing the same. He had vowed to stop their project, to go to city hall about them. Now, with the camera rolling, he had the perfect opportunity to make his point. Why hadn't he spoken up yet?

He snorted. His mouth worked. But he said nothing. Jess caught a flustered look on his face. *Television!* it seemed to say. *I'm on television!*

"He's can't speak!" whispered Cary happily.

146

"He's overwhelmed," said Vivian. "This is too much for him, the camera and everything."

Ramon snickered. "It didn't hurt that Penny Allbright and Mr. Sobieski told him off. He knows he's outnumbered."

Sienna whispered back, "We're famous. On TV. How can he fight TV?"

Mr. Wartman gave one last *harrumph,* then turned and retreated into his house.

"He might as well wave a white flag!" crowed Ramon.

Jess sighed, half in relief and half in frustration. There would always be some people, she realized, like Mr. Wartman, who just wouldn't understand what the Eco-kids were trying to do. Maybe they had won the battle against him, but the important thing was whether or not the Eco-kids could win the war.

The camera turned to Freddy.

"We're going live now," he said, smiling. "Okay, Eco-kids?"

Mutely, Jess nodded. Freedom straightened the WEAR-ING BUTTONS IS NOT ENOUGH button on his lapel. Vivian looked mortified by the prospect of live television. Sienna fluffed her hair.

The camerawoman gave them a three-two-one signal with her fingers.

Following the count of one, Freddy opened with, "In this normal, tree-lined neighborhood, instead of watching cartoons or tossing a softball, saving the earth is what kids do on Saturday mornings."

The camera moved to Webb, Hallie, Patti, and Gina, who were hauling the McCabes' cans, bottles, and newspapers from across the street.

147

Jess smiled at the thought of her family's trash being on TV.

Other neighbors gathered. Around the Eco-kids and reporting crew stood Penny and the Sobieski family, Ramon's mother, Ms. Sanchez, and even Sienna's friend Mandy Sykes who ''wasn't into'' animal and environment stuff. They looked on while Freddy narrated the whole procedure of sorting the recyclables in the collection area, then turned to ask the Sobieskis what they thought of the recycling program. Before the couple could answer, their little son, Jason, grabbed the microphone and licked it like an ice cream cone. Not to miss out on anything good, his older sister, Kimmie, grabbed it for a try. Cary's younger brother, Luke, and his friend Sam stepped in to help Freddy get the mike back. Several seconds of live television passed before he did.

Later, as he wrapped up his report, Freddy looked even more flustered than Mr. Wartman. He yanked a handkerchief from his jacket pocket and mopped his forehead. Jess thought he looked ready to pack up, run away, and forget about filming for the evening news.

Nate, one of the new kids, came up and tugged on Jess's sleeve. ''Look at this.'' He stooped to pick up a few items of litter at their feet—a potato chip bag, a candy bar wrapper, an egg carton. ''This place is a mess.''

Freddy swung toward him.

''It's not *our* mess,'' Cary retorted. ''We always pick up after ourselves on neighborhood recycling days.''

Ramon nodded. ''Everyone else tosses stuff here. People think this is kind of a handy neighborhood minidump.''

Sheela, the sixth grader, said, ''Yeah, but we're the

Eco-kids, right? Maybe we should do something about this.''

Nate nodded. ''If we're going to clean up the earth, why not start in our own neighborhoods?''

Jess saw Freddy motion for the camera to roll. ''I'll pitch in first,'' he said. ''Consider this my first contribution.'' He gathered an armful of trash from the ground and dropped it into an empty wheelbarrow.

Wordlessly, one by one, the Eco-kids, Eco-juniors, and some of the neighbors joined in. Even Mandy Sykes plucked a few gum wrappers and bottle caps out of the weeds. Soon they fanned out across the lot, clearing it of litter.

''Maybe this will make Mr. Wartman happy,'' remarked Vivian.

Cary shook her head. ''Nothing will make Mr. Wartman *happy*.''

But the litter cleanup did make Freddy and the camerawoman happy.

''Great shots,'' she said. ''Got some good stuff.''

Glancing around at all the activity, Jess suddenly understood something important. The vacant lot used to be a place for her and Cary and Sienna to hang out and goof off. Sometimes they'd play games, and sometimes they'd just stand around and argue about what to do next. It was all very different now. The Eco-kids had changed not only her and her friends. The effect was spreading. The word was out.

Cary walked up to collect a crumpled cookie box near Jess. ''Can you believe this response? Neighbors and people from all over the city helping out?''

''It could go even farther!'' Sienna gushed. ''The

149

state, the country, the whole world! Who knows? Eco-kids everywhere!''

Webb wandered over. ''What's this? Eco-kids what?''

Ramon grinned. ''Our next club name. Eco-kids Everywhere. I like it.''

''Hmm.'' Jess chose her words with care. ''Don't you think there's still plenty to do right here in our own town before we branch out?''

''Well, someday we can do it,'' said Sienna. ''We can have a really big, national club. I mean, if adults can have stuff like Greenpeace and the Sierra Club, why can't we go national, too?''

''No reason.'' Cary shrugged. ''Someday.''

Jess sighed contentedly. It was awfully nice to be able to discuss future plans without arguing.

She mouthed the words. *Eco-kids Everywhere*. That possibility seemed pretty far away. There was so much to do first.

She had to admit, though, she sure liked the sound of it.